LONE STARS

LONE
STARS

SOPHIA HEALY

THE ATLANTIC MONTHLY PRESS
NEW YORK

Published simultaneously in Canada

Printed in the United States of America

Library of Congress Cataloging-in-Publication Data

Healy, Sophia.
  Lone stars.

  I. Title.
PS3558.E4586L66   1988   813'.54   88-8070
ISBN 0-87113-302-4

DESIGN BY LAURA HOUGH

The Atlantic Monthly Press
19 Union Square West
New York, NY 10003

FIRST PRINTING

for Alba,
with deep thanks to
Kris and Jules

Nagi leżałem na brzegach
Bezludnych wysp.

Naked I lay on the shores
Of uninhabited islands.

—*Czesław Miłosz*

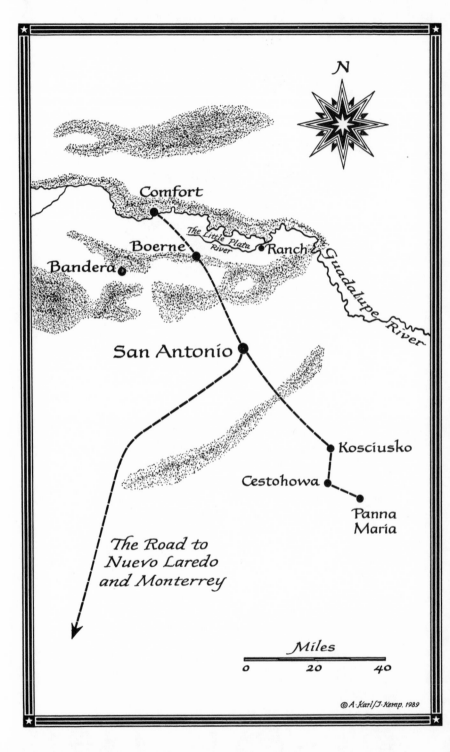

STAŚ

NEW GAINS

Staś had to admit that he felt out of place. He sat in the backyard of Lupe's family's house in San Antonio, reading Conrad's *The Congo Diary*, occasionally nodding and acknowledging Lupe's relatives with a perfect Northern Mexican accent, as they entered and left the house. But he felt out of place with the pecan tree, the lime tree, the banana plant, the two white dogs, both of whom were named Pinky. He felt empathy only for Lupe's older sister, who did not even look up as she greeted him and said, "Staś, it is good to see you, how was the drive?" He felt somehow like Lupe's older sadder sister, who had been divorced by a husband she cared for. *Ella sufre,* he thought . . . she suffers. The Polish turns of phrase, the awkward placement of words, in Conrad's English also comforted him.

He looked at the fan-tail palm in the corner of the yard. How brilliant and exuberant it seemed in the sun, like a dark green comb splayed in Lupe's blue-black hair. He remembered photographing her against this palm five years ago on the day they were married. How stunning an accessory the palm and his wife had seemed for each other—each was the other's chief ornament.

Recently, Staś had begun to speculate in the stock market. The neat columns in the newspaper, the migrating flocks of type, informed him each week of new gains, and from one week to the next he accumulated more and more money, but always an abstract kind of money to be reinvested in the next speculative venture. At this rate, at $7,000 a week, we will have $42,000 in six weeks, he thought, which is more than I used to make in a year. But he remained slightly ill, poorly dressed, disinterested in most things that gave others joy—drinking, dancing, drugs.

His wife's cousin, Faustino, had come from Mexico, and Lupe's excited delivery of the news of this arrival instantly jammed his mind with an unpleasantly accelerated preview of a movie where the characters ate, danced and drank too much. Staś wanted instead to spend the entire week sitting in the yard immersed in Conrad, emerging only to attend a movie theatre in town where a film starring one of the great Mexican actresses, like Lucha Villa, would be playing, and afterwards in the dark rustling theatre, a group of musicians would enter from stage left, and with bright discordant trumpets and an agile accordion, they would accompany a young Mexican boy, at the most age eleven, who would bray out love songs that someone twice his age should be feeling and singing. Perhaps this is how it is with me, Staś thought: My feelings and my song are too mature, too old for my heart.

YOU ARE LIKE
HEALTH

Staś wanted to get a newspaper, the *Wall Street Journal*. Lupe scolded him: What could the stock market possibly do in the week between Christmas and the New Year? "And why not relax for the week?" she asked. Besides, she had a fever. Her mother, Concepción, had just given her some pills. Staś listened politely to the usual comments from every member of the family. When the discussion was finished, they all piled into the car and drove out South Flores Street on the south side of San Antonio. A few children dressed for church hurried along, mostly Hispanics; a few Anglos. Pieces of paper blew across the streets. Staś drove into an aging shopping plaza and parked in front of the supermarket. He put two quarters into a vending machine and got his paper. The family vanished into the store. Staś leaned against the dirt-green Buick and scanned the rows of figures in the bright sun. The shifting figures were like the surface of the river that ran by Staś and Lupe's own house. The river rose and fell, sweeping away familiar things—plants and at times whole trees, banks of earth—and as it washed these away, it brought new vegetation and new configurations. He remembered that after one period of high water, Lupe had found an iris deposited in their yard by the flood. Over the years, this iris had multiplied to become a whole colony of plants, which Lupe weeded as ferociously as her flower beds.

Lupe often asked him, Why don't you do all your trading with your discount broker? Staś pointed out that one needed a personal broker close to the floor, right in the thick of it, responsive to every change in trading activity, changes that could occur as swiftly as the fluctuations in the river. It was like harnessing the tides.

Later in the day Staś stood with Faustino in the kitchen, watching Lupe and her mother make the tamales. Faustino told the funny story of how he had been sent by a gossipy aunt to spy on the family, and to report back to her on it. First Lupe and Concepción made the bean tamales, then the meat, and finally the sugar tamales, with coconut and raisins. Lupe's family liked and admired Staś. Who else could make $7,000 in a week, they asked, without doing anything but read the paper. Proudly Lupe explained to her mother and father how Staś studied the stock market. "It is just like when he goes fishing with his friend Maciej," she said. "Those two sit in the boat studying the cross currents, and then, pop, they throw out the line, and there's always a fish."

That night Staś lay in bed reading Conrad's *The Sisters,* generally acknowledged to be a failed work, but one that he loved because of the infant hero's yearning for the stars. Especially dear to him was the passage describing the small lakes, the dark willows, the slim birches, the sturdy oaks, and the scattered white huts on the slopes leading down into the town. Staś lay back on his pillow, closed his eyes, and listened to his own voice, his voice as a child, recite the first few pages of *Pan Tadeusz:* "*Litwo! Ojczyzno moja! ty jesteś jak zdrowie. . . .*" Staś turned in bed, and reached over to touch Lupe's forehead. During the night her fever broke. He put his arms around her, and whispered, "Lithuania, my country, you are like health."

THE EGG

"**M**other, do the egg on him," Staś heard his wife ask. Now Staś lay in bed, every joint aching. Lupe had rubbed his knees, his lower back, and his scalp, just as he had for her a few nights ago when she had the flu. His mother-in-law, Concepción, came into the bedroom, and with her kind, indefatigable hands, which did so many tasks every day, she wrapped the egg in her blouse and pressed it against her body to warm it in the cold room. She was still sleepy, and hadn't brushed out her hair, allowing a white part to show above her ear. *"Una bruja,* Staś," she laughed at herself. "No, no, not like a witch," he told her. She made two passes, the sign of the cross, over herself, and then began moving the egg in the motions of the cross over his body. The egg thumped over his ribs. She took special care with the lower abdominal region, a part of the body Staś hardly ever considered. But of course, he thought, there are so many precious organs there. When she reached the extremities, she flicked the malevolent energy off her fingers, off the tips of his toes and fingers. With no embarrassment at all, she worked down through his body, again concentrating on the pelvis, where it ached so much. She motioned for him to turn over. He lay with his face in the pillow and felt the fever leaving him. *"Por la calentura y por el ojo.* For the fever and for the evil eye," Concepción told him. He felt Concepción cover him with three thick cotton blankets, and a moment later she returned, with the egg broken into a glass of water and already hazily settling halfway down into the glass, which she put under his bed.

Soon Staś fell asleep and began to dream that he was in an airplane. In his reverie, he tucked his newspaper into the pocket on the seat in front of him. As the plane lifted off he made the sign of the cross over his forehead and chest. Soon the plane broke through the clouds into the blue empyrean, leaving the dirty air and the landscape below. Here, everything was as Staś remembered it from childhood. These must be those flocks that the biblical David kept, he thought, as he looked out at the fantastic fluffy hills and trees and groves, mountains and sheep, all made of white vapor.

He was so glad to be here, and not below in that world where he had struggled painfully as an artist. No one had taken an interest in Staś's paintings: No dealers, no collectors—even other artists seemed perplexed by them. Staś tried to make his paintings as transparent and clear as possible. He wanted to make paintings about nothingness— pure nothingness. To Staś, these paintings presented the same brilliant and perplexing surface as life itself, as love, as the river Guadalupe, as the hand-drawn trading charts he prepared every day of his transactions on the market. Everything seemed an emerging surface from which one could draw only a few conclusions. But the fashion was for a different kind of painting and Staś had not been successful. Presumptuously, he often felt like Cézanne. At first Staś had been hurt by the failure of his art to gain esteem, but then he found new ways to support Lupe and himself. His paintings, a venture now freed entirely from considerations of the art market, multiplied silently in his studio.

He gazed out into the fresh world outside the gray body of the plane, and saw the egg yolk and white scattering, dispersing into the glass of water, sucking away his pain, his years, and he slept again like a child.

THE
COCKATOO

Staś woke up shivering. Pulling his jacket over his pajamas, he went into the kitchen and heated up some *menudo* which he ate with chopped onions, lemon, and a corn tortilla, as his wife had instructed him before she went shopping. Then he sat in the living room, wrapped himself in a blanket, and watched Carmela *y* Rafael on the TV, with Lupe's father. "Carmela *y* Rafael, him live in French," his father-in-law said. "Him never go back to Mexico." They began to discuss the beauty of the old couple, still singing love songs at sixty. "Like me and my wife," his father-in-law said.

Staś began to wonder if he and Lupe would still sing love songs to each other when they were old. Before Staś met Lupe, he and Gosia, an art dealer from Houston, had been lovers for nearly twenty years. They had decided to call it a day when Staś married Lupe. Though he and Gosia remained friends, the change weighed on him. And today, due perhaps to his fever, Staś felt anxious about Lupe. Was there any reason to doubt that he and Lupe would be together forever? Staś tried rephrasing it: Why shouldn't we be together forever? I'm forty-six and Lupe's twenty-six, Staś thought. They had an arrangement: Because of the difference in their ages, they had decided to have affairs with other people if they felt like it, but not to tell each other. Sometimes Lupe stayed away till late at night at the university where she taught. At those times, Staś's heart grew heavy as the evenings went by, and he sat at home. But other times he was quite content with his books and figures. Was Lupe faithful to him? Staś wondered. Or was she having an affair at the university? Staś put his hand to his head; his hair was still damp with fever. He stood up, walked back into his bedroom, lay down on the bed and pondered a dream he had told his analyst. The woman in the dream was older, like his former mistress, Gosia, but she had dark hair like Lupe.

When Staś's family first came from Poland to Washington, D.C., they lived with a wealthy relative in a large house which had a pantry and a laundry room with two set-tubs. The dream took place in this laundry room. Staś was a little boy. Several women were ironing sheets. A white mist and the flapping of white sheets filled the air, which combined erotically with the steamy smell of the sheets and the women. Suddenly one of the laundresses, a tall one, leaned over to raise the height of the ironing board. As she did so, a green cockatoo, which had been sitting on the crossbraces, flew up and fluttered about the ceiling before finding a perch on top of a curtain. The women in the room were startled by the cockatoo and scurried about, white sheets flying. At this moment, Staś experienced his first sexual excitement. "What do you think of that?" Staś had asked his analyst. "Is the woman Gosia or Lupe?" "I don't know," his analyst replied. "The question is, what is the cockatoo?" "You're quite the wag," Staś said.

ANYTHING
MAY BE
DONE, BUT
WITH CAUTION

Staś still felt hot and cold. He sat up in bed, opened his briefcase, and looked through the confirmation slips from his broker. There was the Texaco he had bought at 29 and sold at 31, the Merrill Lynch he had bought at 36 and sold at 38. He stuffed the slips into an envelope to send to his accountant. He rummaged around in the briefcase and found the little Mexican toy he had picked up in Nuevo Laredo. Two boxers faced each other. When you pressed a little tab of wood on the base, the boxers began to punch at each other with short jabs. Staś decided to send this boxing toy to his friend Vassily.

Vassily was from Leningrad. In another life, in a White Russia, Vassily would have been a diplomat, Staś thought. But in the U.S., he was a music producer with a sideline in cocaine. Staś, Vassily and Gosia had been friends for a long time. Like other exiles of their acquaintance, they were surviving in America by means of their cleverness and wits, without doing very much. Gosia lived by ingratiating herself with wealthy people. She was always being offered a yacht or house to live in, rent-free. Gosia made the rich feel that they were interesting and intelligent by the very fact of their having invited her to stay on their yacht, or in their spare country home. When she moved to Houston with the idea of opening an art gallery, Staś and Vassily followed. It was at Gosia's gallery, La Arena, that Staś first met Lupe, when Gosia showed Lupe's work in a group exhibit called "Young Texas." Although Vassily had worked briefly for Gosia in her gallery, he had decided not to settle down in Houston, but to travel around the world as was usual for him. Staś, who in Poland would probably have made a career as an army officer, had ended up making his living in the U.S. by speculating in the market—playing the grand casino of history, as he used to say.

Staś and Vassily had met at a prep school in Washington, which many émigré children attended. The melancholy Pole and the ineffable Russian had become friends instantly. Staś's parents used to refer to Staś and Vassily as "Pushkin and Mickiewicz." Both remained romantic in temperament, Vassily always in search of the indescribable, and Staś deepening in melancholy as he grew older. Only Gosia had changed. Was it the opium in the ivory pipe, the rich meats, the vodka, the cigarettes she clenched between her dazzling white teeth? As Gosia had grown older, her beauty had changed to a rare handsomeness. When the two young men had first met Gosia, she was slender, beautiful, impetuous. Dmitri, Vassily's brother, had met Gosia first, at a party. She attacked Dmitri in the coatroom as he was leaving. Dmitri had gone into the bedroom where the coats were, and Gosia had tried to rape him, as he put it. Since he was a womanizer, he wasn't able to tolerate such an advance, but he wanted Vassily and Staś to meet her, because she was a true beauty.

"Of course Dmitri wouldn't respond to such a overture," Staś told Vassily, *"Wszystko można, lecz z ostrożna."*

"Mozhno—no ostorozhno," Vassily said. "Anything may be done, but with caution."

Soon Vassily and Gosia met, and became friends. Gosia knew someone in the country, in Vermont, who had a house. Staś met Gosia for the first time on the morning that all three of them left Washington for a hunting weekend in the country. Polish women know how to dress beautifully, and Gosia was no exception. Staś was immediately attracted by her height, and the very Polish beauty of her highly arched eyebrows and full lips. They had a delightful trip in the car, and after each of them had unpacked in their separate rooms, they set out into the fields.

Gosia was very handsome in her whipcord pants and rough corduroy jacket. Staś recalled that she had worn a silk shirt beneath a light wool sweater. She was perfectly dressed for a grouse hunt. Vassily had decided not to go out with a gun. He brought a wicker basket from the house, and took off in an opposite direction to look for mushrooms, some of which he hoped would produce the extraordinary effects he always sought. Staś elected to tramp about in the small thickets, and in the grassy hollows, to scare up a few birds for Gosia, who followed along behind him. Soon Staś wandered into a thicket and absentmindedly became absorbed in the beauty of the poplar grove he stood in. Suddenly he remembered his companion, and returned to the meadow and started to climb a rise. At the top he ran into Gosia, who lifted her shotgun instinctively, muzzle towards him.

"Don't shoot," he cried. "Let's sit down here and rest." They sat in a patch of soft grass that had been bent sideways by the wind, or by deer lying there. Staś leaned back and fell asleep in the autumn sunlight. He often fell asleep for a few minutes when he was content.

He was awoken, as any young man would dream to be awoken, by the pressure of Gosia's lips on his, her body against him. She had taken off her whipcord pants, and her very long white legs glistened in the sun. He felt immediate and serious desire. How often he had swiftly slipped off his trousers to make love. How well he recognized, in himself, her sudden rash haste. They made love in the grass, and he felt the rabbits going down into the earth beneath him, somewhere deep in their hollows. He felt the wind ruffle his hair, as if he were a fox pausing on a knoll, to sense the wind. They made love as if they were one person united again, like two halves of a nut that needed only to be rejoined.

In this way began a relationship that was to last twenty years, through Gosia's marriage and her affairs, and through Staś's affairs, until his marriage. They fought if they ever had to spend more than half an hour together without making love. They were too similar to live with each other, but they had to have each other. They made love in bedrooms at parties, on the kitchen floor of friends' houses while waiting for the friends to return, in cars, on sofas, in carriages, on yachts, in country houses, in city houses.

And now this was all over. The unraveling of the passion between himself and Gosia made him feel deeply sad. Who could tell what life might bring at any moment, Staś thought. He laid back in bed and thought about Lupe again. As Lupe had laughingly noted, he, Staś, was hardly the *gringo* of her adolescent dreams. She had once told him that she had wanted to marry a real white guy, someone who installed satellite dishes for a living, and who would always seem to know exactly how much life could give him. "But you, Staś, knowing you and your friends . . . you're all living on luck."

BIEN COCIDO

Staś had been watching the Financial News Network. It was the big thing in Texas, everyone sat mesmerized in front of their sets. Narrowcasting they called it. FNNI. He looked it up on the NASDAQ Supplemental list, and found it had last traded at 7 to 7½. He decided to call his broker later and buy 2,000 shares. He studied the penny stocks. If he had bought 15,000 Nastech Pharmaceutical shares for $5,000 on April 4, he would have $656,250 today.

What should he think about? His mother-in-law came in with her short little steps, and got the glass from under his bed. *"Bien cocido . . .* well cooked," she said, *"por la calentura."* By the fever. She showed him the glass with the egg in it which had settled overnight. The egg had dropped two-thirds of the way down into the water. The yolk looked like a melancholy sun. The white had congealed into a wide ring about the yolk, set at about twenty-three degrees off its axis. Staś murmured, *"Gracias a ti, madre."* She left the room. Now what should he think about? Staś decided to think about two things at once. Clearly the stock market was like the rippling skin of the panther that was America. Also he concentrated on the dark sun he had just seen. It was like the earth, but from a distance it might look like a disk, or a void, like the hollow of an instrument, surrounded by a bright ring—the ornament around the sounding hole. Staś felt pleasantly insulated from the chatter coming distantly from the kitchen. Lupe had stuffed his ears with cotton before she left in the morning to move her sister's VCR over to her parents' house. But the two topics deserted Staś. A movie seemed to be playing in his head. Someone was threatening someone else. They had better hand over three thousand dollars, or else. Staś fell into sleep.

MORTALITY: OR, THE CALL FROM MONTERREY

"When are you leaving for the ranch?" his mother-in-law called from the next room.

"The day after tomorrow," Lupe answered from under the bedcovers, beside Staś.

About noontime the telephone rang. It was from Mexico. His mother-in-law began to talk happily, but then she burst into tears. "Ay, Juanita is dead. No, no, Rubén," she cried. Staś got up and walked around the bedroom, and began to cry. His mother-in-law came in, and they embraced each other and sobbed long sobs into each others' hair. "Mustn't be sad, Stachi," Concepción said. "Now she sleeping."

Staś remembered their last visit to Monterrey. Rubén's wife, Juanita, had hobbled brightly around the kitchen like a cricket; she was very tiny, a Veracruzana. Arthritis had almost crippled her completely. Her limbs were crooked and thin as bone, and her legs were entirely purple and white with scale. Staś remembered Juanita turning this way and that, very painfully and slowly, to show off her small waist. "They used to call me Coca," she said. "When I came from Veracruz, I was so thin, like a Coca-Cola bottle, but above, I was big. They called me 'the grapes.' " Juanita had given Lupe a lovely gift, a black serape inwoven with silver. "Wear this for me. Dance for me," Juanita said, and she had executed a few turning steps in her kitchen.

Lupe didn't want to talk about Juanita. Staś thought: She'll cry this evening. "Why don't we go to the mall," he suggested. "We'll look for a ring for you." In the long light alleys of the mall, Lupe walked along with Staś, holding his hand. They stopped to examine a silk jacket. Staś tried it on, but they decided it was not well-enough made for the price. While Lupe went into a little store to look for a sale, Staś walked into a jeweler's and found a gold ring with a cluster of small diamonds and one bigger diamond, very bright in its color, in the center. "Lupe," he called when he saw her walking past in the crowd. She came in smiling. "Mmm, it's very pretty. We'll come back tomorrow," she decided.

Then they drove downtown to the *mercado,* where they bought gifts to take to friends, and Lupe bought a little scene for herself. Made of thin sticks of light wood, only big enough to fit into Lupe's hand, a complete tableau was assembled. There were two tiny rabbits in a vegetable garden, a swing set, a little girl on the swing, and a little boy watching from the side. The children's faces were painted like skulls: For their teeth, black lines were painted over a glaring white. In every other way the toy was pleasing and brightly colored. This is like a Watteau, or what? Staś thought. When they got home, he decided to finish his book before returning to their ranch. He was reading the part about the Spanish couple who lived in Passy. But Conrad's leisurely pace immediately slowed Staś down, and he found he could only read one or two pages at a time before feeling deliciously sated.

THE TRIP TO PANNA MARIA

The next day Staś and Lupe felt completely recovered from their flu. "Come on, Mother, Staś is going to take us to Panna Maria," Lupe said.

"The shrine?" Concepción asked.

"No, not the shrine. You know, that little town where Staś likes to talk to the old men in the store."

Every year they made the trip to the Polish settlements below San Antonio. Usually they stopped at the shrine of Our Lady of Częstochowa on Beethoven Street on their way out of San Antonio, but this year Staś headed straight out Route 37 to 181.

"What time is it?" Staś asked.

"Seven *jalapeños* before eleven, didn't you hear the radio announcer?" Lupe asked.

"Ah, we're making good time," Staś said. "Now tell me this plan you two have to make money in Mexico."

"I don't know, what is it, Mother?" Lupe asked, "How is it we're making money?"

Concepción explained in Spanish, and then in English. "First I travel across the border to see my sister. Then I return to San Antonio to explain to my family how the Mexican government needs U.S. dollars. I take one thousand U.S. dollars. Lupe gave me two hundred of this. I go back on the bus and put the thousand dollars in the bank, and in three months time we receive three hundred dollars interest in pesos. No, a little less."

"Just a little less," Lupe said.

"True?" Staś asked.

"It's true, and we're helping Mexico in this way."

"Like Robin Hood, Pancho Villa," Staś said.

Staś listened to Lupe explain the story of Robin Hood to Concepción as they drove along, and remembered the first time he saw the great Lucha Villa in a film. The audience heard her voice, but saw only her back as she sang. Staś was so absorbed in his thoughts, waiting for the moment when Lucha Villa would turn at the end of the song to show her magnificent sad face, that Lupe was the first to see the steeple of the large church at Kosciusko rising from the flat green of the live oaks.

"The church is always such a surprise," Staś said, "like coming upon a familiar sight in outer space."

They pulled into the circular turn-around beside the Dworaczyk Market, and sat in the car, looking at the church and the market.

"Is the market open?" Lupe asked.

"It looks as if it's closed," Staś said, "it's sad." In Texas, each of these Polish towns was the same, Staś thought: a church in the middle of nowhere, depopulated, *despoblado*.

They drove on to Cestohowa, a few miles to the south, and walked around the grounds. Concepción wanted to see the cross in front of the church.

"This cross was brought from Poland," Staś explained, "and it used to be placed way at the top of the first church they built here in 1878." Concepción nodded.

"Look Mother, here's the shrine of the two Virgins," Lupe said. They entered the limestone grotto. Staś, Lupe and Concepción barely fit inside at once. The Madonna of Częstochowa and the Virgin of Guadalupe stood in separate niches, illumined by the lights of flickering candles. Concepción drew in her breath. "*La patrona de México y la patrona de Polonia,*" she said. They lit small red candles, and Staś placed quarters in the metal slots below the tiers of candles. Again, inside the church, they lit more candles. As they left the church, Concepción blessed the back of Lupe's neck with holy water from the font beside the door.

Concepción started to talk about the pope. "The pope is actually God," Concepción explained, when they were back in the car. "That's why he has such delicate features— that's why his voice isn't like other men's voices."

Now they were approaching their destination, Panna Maria. When Staś saw the spire of Panna Maria, he pulled off the highway onto a side road, and in less than a minute they were parked before the rectangular storefront which was lettered across the top F. V. SNOGA.

"There's the oak where the first hundred families arrived from Poland," Staś explained. "They were so tired from walking across Texas from the sea that they fell asleep, and then at midnight they said their first Mass. This is the first continuous Polish settlement in the U.S.A., *Madre*."

"*¡AY!*" Concepción said, and again she drew her breath in, even though Staś told her this story every year.

Concepción and Lupe got out of the car and walked around the oak and went into the church. Staś walked along the road to visit the old woman who lived on a side road not far from the church. She was eighty-two, and her skin had been thickened and browned by the sun. Staś liked to hear her tell the story of how she had moved to Panna Maria when she was a young girl. Staś split some wood for her, and then he went back to the store. Lupe and Concepción sat at a table in back having Cokes. "Don't bother him, Mother," Lupe said, "he wants to talk Polish."

Staś sat down with the men. "How was your corn crop, Felix?" Staś asked. "Hello Staś," everyone said, recognizing him. They settled into a conversation about the weather and the crops, hardly different from the conversation they had had the previous year. Staś nodded once in a while to Lupe and Concepción, who seemed to be watching him with pride, although perhaps, he thought, Lupe finds me a little silly. Or old-fashioned?

That evening, when Staś lay down in bed, Lupe asked, "Do you always have to lie down like a tamale?"

"What?" Staś asked.

"When you sit down on the bed, you fold yourself up like a tamale, then . . . whack . . . you lie down as if you're wrapped in a corn husk. You're just a big tamale."

Staś laughed.

THE RETURN
TO THE
RANCH

Staś spent the next morning working on his Buick's carburetor. He sat at the kitchen table with his father-in-law. A cold front had moved into San Antonio at midnight, and the day was clear and blue. After lunch, Staś and Lupe decided to leave for their ranch, as Concepción called it. Actually their property was just a house and a barn on five acres of land along a branch of the Guadalupe River. As they departed, Concepción shut the gate to the yard behind them, and embraced Staś and Lupe. "*Vayan con Dios*, goodbye Stachi," she said. "God bless."

"Turn the radio back to 1540, *amor*," Staś said, "*Radio Jalapeño . . . peño . . . peño . . . música caliente.*" He tried to imitate the echo-chamber effect the Mexican station used for its advertisement. The sobbing voice of Cornelio Reyna filled the car. Lupe began to sing, "*. . . me caí de la nube que andaba . . .* I fell from the cloud . . ." as they drove along

South Flores Street past the BAR-B-Q BARREL, where the owner made barbecue grills from old oil drums, past the school-supply store, and out onto the expressway.

"It's certainly a wonder how I've come to be here," Staś said. "I didn't choose Texas; it called me."

"Remember how we met at Gosia's gallery?" Lupe turned down the radio.

"That's right, you were so beautiful. I couldn't believe my eyes. I feel in love immediately. You were in that exhibition of emerging talent, or 'Young Texas,' as Gosia called it."

"You told me you were Polish. I had never met anyone Polish before you and Gosia. All I could think of was the Texas Folklife Fair and some wood carvings. I had never seen Our Lady of Częstochowa."

They turned out onto IH-10 and headed towards Boerne. Something on the bottom of the car was shaking in the wind. It made a little clacking sound as they went along. They passed the university where Lupe taught. "I'm excited to get home," Lupe said.

"*Zmienność* . . . our property," Staś said. He liked to call the land they lived on "*Zmienność*," or "Mutability," as if it were an estate.

"Hmmmm," Lupe said.

They passed the miles of brown grass, the ranches, the clumps of live oaks, the turn off to Boerne where Staś had his painting studio, and swung off to the right onto the narrow ranch road that led to their house. The car raised a trail of dust behind it as they went down the road towards the river. The green Buick clattered slowly over the wooden bridge. A gray Honda was parked in front of their house, alongside of Staś's '59 Dodge, under the pecan trees.

"Whose is that?" Lupe asked.

"Maciej. He probably borrowed a car at the university. He's here to feed the cats."

"Maciej, your other you," Lupe said.

Staś parked the car and Lupe immediately got out and carried something into the kitchen, scolding the cats who came out to greet her as she walked along.

Staś sat in the cooling car, and listened to the metal tick. He could faintly hear Maciej and Lupe talking in the kitchen. Maciej came out, followed by the big black dog with graying whiskers that belonged to both Maciej and Staś.

"Babka," Staś said. He climbed out of the car and greeted the old dog. "My *owczarek,* my lovely sheepdog," he said. "Good morning, Babka." Babka stretched out her front paws and bowed stiffly. The two men stood talking in the sunlight. Babka watched them for awhile, and then lay down in the dust.

"What are you going to do this weekend?" Staś asked.

"I'm going to Bandera. I met an old lady there who turns out to be a distant cousin. Anna Przygoda. Then I'm going down to Panna Maria."

"We were just there," Staś said.

"Well then, perhaps Babka will come with me," Maciej said. Babka stood up and walked over beside Maciej. Maciej bent down and stroked her shoulders.

"Yes, take Babka, and bring her back in a few weeks— when Lupe's show goes up in Houston I'll want her here with me."

"For sure," Maciej said. He opened the front door of the gray car and patted the upholstery. Babka bounded forward and climbed onto the seat, and looked back at Staś.

Staś watched as the car drove away across the bridge. Then he walked down to the grove of ash-leaf maples by the river and tested his weight with his hands on the string hammock that hung between two of the older trees. He climbed into the hammock and fell asleep.

LUPE

PENSANDO

Lupe busied herself in the kitchen unpacking the chiles that her mother had given her. She started some laundry in the machine. Then she went outdoors to check everything in the yard. She walked over to the bridge. The branch of the river Guadalupe that they lived on was called the Little Plata, and the water shone like silver in the sun. She looked across the bridge at the bald cypresses shedding bark in long pale strips into the river. Lupe loved the murmur of the water as it passed over and around the white rocks. Staś was asleep in the hammock by the trees. The cats too were asleep on the warm hood of the Buick. She turned back to the house and stopped to look for the red fruit on the *nopalitos* growing by the side of the small steep-roofed barn where they kept their tools. Buttoning her coat, she examined the brown-and-yellow '59 Dodge parked under the trees and decided to walk around their property.

Even though the yard was brown with dry grass, much

of their property appeared as an oasis because they had brought in topsoil for the gardens, and planted many trees—*bananos* by the clothesline, fig and peach trees, and crepe myrtles on the west side of the house. The house faced south to catch the cooling winds. Lupe walked up to one of the crepe myrtles and pressed her face against the smooth bark, bark which always felt to her like skin. She walked around behind the house and sat on a rock. She never seemed to be able to concentrate while Staś was around, but now that he was asleep, she could think clearly. She looked out over their back fence at the pasture, the mesquite and the live oaks receding into the distance. A few tall ash-leaf maples along the fenceline were all that remained of a windbreak planted years ago by the first settlers. Along the far east side of their property, standing cornstalks glistened in the sunlight. In front of her was her little round herb garden, and to the right of it, Staś's flat rectangular garden. Her garden was shaped like a mound, with rocks and earth, cilantro, chile piquín, and cacti in the center, and medicinal shrubs all around it. One cactus that she had smuggled in from Mexico grew near the top rocks; it was shaped exactly like a breast emerging from the earth.

Lupe wished that she could sit here with some little children, and put the herbs under their noses. But Staś wouldn't like it. Even when they had lived at her parents' house, when they were first married, Staś had seemed jealous of the neighborhood children who were always visiting Concepción and Lupe in the kitchen. Staś would look irritated when he came home and saw Concepción and Lupe with the little ones on their laps, having just cured them with the egg or some linden tea. All the neighbors brought their children, but out here on the ranch no neighbors ever brought their children to have their fevers magically reduced. Lupe reached for a stick and scratched a small circle in her herb garden.

She turned to look at the house. It was such a simple house—a kitchen, a dining room, a living room, and their bedroom. All the rooms opened onto a porch that ran the length of the back side of the house, and in the summer they moved tables, chairs and beds out onto the porch, and ate and slept on the porch. And sometimes, on very hot nights, they climbed up the ladder and slept on the porch roof. Lupe couldn't help smiling as she looked up at the roof, now littered with pecan leaves, because she remembered the hot night they had made love under the stars and the pecan tree, and had almost rolled off the roof. "Isn't that an expression?" she had asked Staś. "Isn't there an expression you white people use: 'to fall off the roof'?" "I don't know," Staś had said, "I have never heard it." And they had lain in each other's arms while Staś pointed out the drawings in the stars.

Lupe's thoughts were interrupted by the clanking of the rinse cycle of the washing machine. Lupe liked to hang the clothing out in the air. She went into the house, and brought the laundry out to the backyard. "But why is Staś never happy?" Lupe wondered. Even when Staś seemed to be happy, it was just another face of his sadness. But Lupe could be happy, just as she was now, hanging out the clothes on the line. She liked crisply snapping the shirts out into the wind, and filling the clothesline with the parades of wet, vividly colored clothing. Staś often came outdoors to the line, to her, with that crazy camera of his. The camera didn't click till some time after you pushed the button. He would take photos of her laundry, complimenting her on the festive arrangements of colors.

She knew that she was his only happiness, but was he hers? For instance, he was always so big-shot, so *muy macho*. He was always saying things like, "Listen Lupe, I have a play on Phillips Petroleum. We buy 1,000 at 9¼, sell it when it goes up 3 points, meanwhile we pick up that 10 percent dividend on the way." It was always "we this" or "we that." Lupe was proud of him, but her mind was on other things— the movement of the wind in her dress, the way the earth felt under her feet. Staś is a man who wears shoes, Lupe thought.

She remembered the greatest happiness of her life. She yearned to return to those summers of her childhood, in a small Mexican town, far inland. Those summers when it was so hot she and her sisters would lie indoors on the cool floor all day long. And how differently time passed there; time there was like a lizard that paused all day long on a tree trunk, and then quickly darted forward in the evening. Hanging the clothes on the line, she suddenly felt like her mother. When she finished with the laundry, she turned to watch the squirrels in the pecan tree. Two squirrels were playing, circling the tree, with sudden stops and starts.

Everything in nature has children, she thought. But whenever Lupe brought up the matter of children, Staś always said "The last thing I want to do is inflict life on the unborn." And he laughed in that cold unsettling manner of his.

She closed her eyes for a minute and could hear Staś just this morning saying, "Every time I see children I feel sad. They look happy now, but soon they'll grow up and start to feel pain—they'll fall in love. Hardly do they get to know their parents before they die, or their country is taken over by yet another dictator. And shouldn't we be taking care of the little ones that by some misfortune already exist? All those homeless little ones should be adopted before people think of conceiving more. I just feel unremittingly gloomy about this subject, Lupe."

Lupe kept her eyes closed. She tried to picture a world without children in it, no children in their yard, no more people to populate the world, empty streets. Why did Staś have these ideas? Lupe very much wanted to have children. Should she stay with Staś? She felt she ought to. After all, who would take care of him? He was a genius. But was he really a genius? She doubted it. After all, that time on the airplane trip she had correctly answered all the puzzles in the airline magazine. But he just mumbled "seventeen" when she asked him to count all the triangles in the figure presented. She counted carefully and there were thirty-five, which was the proper answer. He was less like a genius than a demon. That's what he was: a demon. He spent half of his days lying in the bedroom studying those stock figures, never making a mistake. That's why he never loses money, Lupe thought: He's a demon.

She certainly did love him in a vivid way. She loved their house on the Little Plata. She loved his melancholy, his long penis reaching into her and touching her; somehow his sadness seemed more real and dear to her than anything else. But he never wanted to do anything spontaneous. He had his own idea of how each day should go, and he seemed to dislike surprises.

A mosquito settled on Lupe's arm and she swatted it. Looking at the mosquito with its narrow nose made her think of Vassily. Once, she had hoped to have an affair with

Vassily. She wished she could phone Vassily today. Vassily seemed to understand her, from the moment they had met. He had taken a beautiful photo of her red dress hanging in a window. He had fussed over this photo of her dress for months, and then sent her a huge print of it. The dress was her heart, her portrait. And Vassily was always so entertaining, so lively, dressing up like a waitress one morning to serve breakfast to her and Staś.

The next time Vassily was in Houston, she planned to visit him for a few days. Lupe suddenly remembered a joke Vassily had told her. A man went into a drugstore, and said to the lady, "I've had an erection for a week, and I can't get rid of it. What can you give me?" The lady said, "The store, and $5,000."

Now why would Vassily tell her a joke like that if he weren't attracted to her? She had responded with Staś's joke about the woman who goes to her broker. The broker says, "The computer's down, but I'm up."

Also, why did Vassily send her a small monster from Japan for Christmas? It was made of some mysterious substance. When you put it into water, it was supposed to swell up to two or three hundred times its size. Staś had said that it would swell up to the size of their bathtub. Why would Vassily give her such a suggestive gift?

Vassily understood her in some way that Staś didn't. But she couldn't phone him because he had gone to spend the first week of January with the Hopi Indians. Then, at Easter, he had said he might go to Spain to travel a few weeks with the gypsies. "I feel most at home with the gypsies," he had said, "with wandering people." Would she really like a life like that, traveling all the time? Perhaps it was better to be with someone like Staś, who could always be counted on to be in the bedroom every night studying those figures, or in the hammock, dreaming.

UNIVERSITY

Lupe thought to herself: Now Staś is looking at the moon, but what's he listening for? Those oil wells? They had been playing racquetball, and as they left the gymnasium they had both paused to look at the moon, which hung over the athletic field. In the dark you could see the elbows of two oil wells at the end of the field going up and down, pumping. Staś dropped Lupe at the art building, and she went to the restroom to change her clothes. She put on spike heels, gray jeans, and a soft purple blouse which she left loose. She drew two delicate black lines under each lower eyelid, and stepped back to study herself in the mirror. She turned sideways. She looked good. Her black hair hung almost all the way down her back. Her back bowed slightly inward in the Spanish manner. She had beautiful breasts, long legs, and light agile hands and feet. Staś always told her she exactly resembled the Duchess of Alba in those drawings by Goya in the

Sanlúcar Álbum, especially the one of the woman greeting the sun.

Should she go to her studio? She had spent all afternoon there, sitting in the studio looking at the space. She decided to go to the library to get another Conrad book for her and Staś to read. They had almost finished *The Shadow-Line.* As she walked along, she again started to think about Staś. In some ways he was a little too much like a Mexican, the way he would come into a house and expect all the women to gather around him. And he wanted all his meals cooked for him, dishes washed. Wouldn't Vassily laugh and put on an apron and help with the dishes after dinner if he were her husband? Vassily was so blond and white; perhaps she could absorb him in some way, the way the Mexican-Americans were reclaiming the Southwest. But how could she get Vassily into bed? This was a problem. In a few weeks she would be in Houston for her exhibition. Could she ask Gosia about it? Would this be something white women did as they hung a show, chat about their problems with men? She tried to picture it. But Gosia always said, "Men, they're so impossible, I could never live with one again." Lupe very much admired Gosia, but how could Gosia say such a thing? The first time Lupe had met Gosia at the gallery, Concepción had whispered in Lupe's ear, "*Una manflora.* This tall woman is a *manflora.* She has the ability to make both men and women love her. She wants to sleep with you, to take you as a lover."

"Oh no, Mother," Lupe had assured Concepción, "she is just very handsome. It's called 'poise.' It's part of her business to be that way."

Actually, Lupe had noticed a subtle current between Gosia and herself. Lupe had heard of such women, *las tortilleras,* and of the rapid patting motions which could cause women to take up with them. Sometimes Gosia seemed to flirt with her, to look deeply into her eyes. Lupe's heart stammered when she thought about lying down in a bed with Gosia. There was a rumor that Gosia already had a lover, an Irish woman who also showed in the gallery. Besides, Lupe thought, could she really ever be with anyone but Staszek? Would anyone else sigh and moan as Staś did? Could anyone find her as beautiful as he did? She didn't know. She laughed to herself excitedly in the cool night, laughing just from a sense of the freshness, the coolness, the exhilaration of the darkening night as she hurried along towards the lights of the library.

EVENING

Lupe hummed as she cooked. She was heating up some chicken *mole,* when the phone rang.

"Oh damn," she said, "hello?"

"Lupe, this is Maciej. Am I disturbing you?"

"No, what's up?"

"Good news, my wife has permission to come from Poland. She'll be here in a few weeks."

"Oh Maciej, you're making me cry. Come on over and have a beer."

"In truth, I'll be right over."

Maciej showed up in half an hour. Lupe was always pleased when Maciej stayed for dinner, because she liked to listen to Maciej and Staś talk about Polish affairs. "Come on into the living room, sit down," Lupe said. "You're going to have dinner with us. We're having chicken with *mole* sauce."

"I'm hungry for that," Maciej said, "Where's Staś?"

"Oh he's been crazy lately. I mean he always is, don't you think? First he sold the computer stock, and then it went up two points. Then he didn't buy some options, and they rose five. Then we had this prospectus around the house for two weeks, and he forgot to call the pennystock broker, and this stock he could have bought for a penny rose to thirty cents a share."

"Maybe he's upset because Gosia is giving you an exhibition," Maciej said.

"He doesn't tell his feelings about such things. I know she only takes his work on consignment, and very rarely. He says he has his mind on other things. Anyway, Staś kept forgetting to act on these stock matters, but then he made a few thousand on some brokerage-firm stock, and he went out and bought a sports car he saw from a bus. He was on the east side, you know, the black part of San Antonio, leaving the Dodge off to replace the master cylinder. They sent the part up from Corpus. He was taking a bus back to my parents' house when he saw the sports car. He jumped off the bus and bought it. He's out in the sports car right now, but he'll be back for supper. This isn't the worst of it, Maciej, the other day I was walking to the parking lot at the university, and I felt like I was missing something. Something in my purse. I got down on the lawn and spread everything out on the grass, my keys, everything. Suddenly that graphics teacher came along, that fellow I assist at the university. I felt embarrassed, so I asked him to dinner. I call Staś, he says fine. We're all out here at the house, and this is the first day Staś bought the car. It's a surprise; Staś isn't gloomy, he's merry. To top it off, Staś says he's going to be on TV that night at 9 P.M. We eat dinner, and everything goes fine until 9. Then Staś turns on the TV. It's

____

46

about the bus. They're changing some bus routes. Suddenly there's Staś. The TV crew gets on the bus, and Staś is sitting there with all these beautiful young black girls. He's leaning against the window, his shirtsleeves rolled up, looking cocky, with a whole busload full of beautiful women. It makes me laugh so hard I have to leave the room. Staś starts laughing too. He has to go outdoors he's laughing so hard. I start to laugh more. Finally I have to go into our bedroom and lay down on the floor to get cool, and I still can't stop laughing. I'm laughing so hard it hurts. Meanwhile the professor is sitting in the living room like a white person, very stiff and stuffy like there's a stick up his ass, looking very polite. Staś tries to stop laughing, but every time he comes through the door, he cracks up again."

Maciej listened thoughtfully. "Well, it is funny," he said.

"I know, Maciej, but can't he ever behave?"

"I don't think so, Lupe, but I know he loves you. And you look wonderful in that blouse. Is it new?"

"It is. You really notice things. Everything's on special at the mall. Do you ever go to Solo Serve?"

"No," Maciej said, "I'm not a shopper. By the way, I stopped by your studio, and your painting is beautiful."

"The red one?"

"Yes, the red one with that green." Maciej lifted his long expressive hands to indicate passages of beauty. He crossed his legs, and leaned back against the sofa. Lupe relaxed, and leaned back too. Twilight entered the room through the windows, and a little wind stirred the partially drawn shades. One of the cats jumped down from a table. A cricket somewhere in the house broke the silence, and then a car roared across the bridge and into the yard. Lupe said, "That's the car."

SUPPER

"What's this?" Staś asked. "Oh, it's a postcard from Vassily, in the desert somewhere. It's a photo of a red rock in the desert. Wasn't he going to Spain to pick up those Man Ray photographs?"

"I don't know where he is," Lupe said, "but that postcard is two weeks old."

"My God, this looks good," Staś exclaimed. He carried the large red earthenware pot into the dining room and set it on the table. This was the very pot Juanita had given them the last time they were in Monterrey. Now the pot was full, with breasts of chicken baked with rice, peppers, garbanzo beans, and steaming brown *mole* sauce. A vase of long-stemmed roses stood in the center of the table.

"I sent these roses to Lupe, and they delivered them right to her studio," Staś said.

"Sit down everyone," Lupe said. "You can get the tortillas out of this napkin."

"It looks so good," Staś said.

"Alright, alright," Lupe said.

The three bowed their heads and Maciej said, "We thank you Lord for bringing us together. And soon my wife."

They began to eat. "Another biologist is coming over from Poland," Maciej said to Lupe.

"Another?" Lupe asked.

"Yes, different from me, very theoretical," Maciej explained. "He went out into the field and found a mite no one had discovered before, *Tarsonemus milosi*. He named it after Miłosz. His book is in press. How do you say that?"

"Being published," Lupe said.

"Oh yes, being published. Anyway, the university is asking him over here."

"And how's your work going?" Lupe asked Maciej.

"Oh, slow, you know. We breed those fruit flies, and watch to see how chemicals affect them genetically. Applied science. We report to the Centers for Disease Control in Atlanta. The best part is devising experiments."

"Exactly," Staś said. "An experiment can be beautiful, like a work of art. Now take Madame Wu. She chills a cobalt atom to a certain temperature, puts it into a magnetic field, and it emits more electrons from the south pole than from the north. Or vice versa. Her experiment is so sensitively devised, it's like playing the Goldberg Variations to do it."

"I don't know," Maciej said, "our work isn't always that fascinating. Sometimes I envy the flash of other people's work."

"I know," Staś said. "It's like the guy who goes to work every day, versus the fellow who plays the market and lives on the line. And speaking of the market, look at this latest Tylenol thing. It's obvious someone is shorting the stock."

"What is that—'shorting'?" Maciej asked.

Lupe explained, "You borrow stock, sell it high. Then the market drops, you buy the stock low, and repay the lender with the stock you bought low. But Staś, that's the craziest idea!"

"No, look Lupe, when the shuttle accident happened, Lockheed dropped 4 points in 10 minutes. A guy I know bought 4,000 shares. When Lockheed went up again he made $16,000. It's ghoulish."

"Well, my idea is that some woman was peeved at her husband. She tries to poison him, but she has to put cyanide in some other bottles of Tylenol to lead the police off the scent."

"No, what it is, is that an employee of Johnson & Johnson is unhappy. He wants to make Johnson & Johnson look bad," Maciej said.

"Well," Staś said, "clearly this Tylenol subject is like a Rorschach test."

"Mmmhmm, that may be, Staś," Lupe said. "But Maciej, isn't it true your brother is publishing a book of Polish poems? Up in Massachusetts?"

"That's right," Maciej said, "the United States is getting more Polish people every day."

Staś continued, "Well, a good experiment should have firmness, commodity and delight. That's what Maciej was telling me last week."

"That's true, Staś," Maciej affirmed. "Those are the qualities Vitruvius believed architecture should have. Only in place of 'commodity,' let's say 'usefulness.' An experiment is not commodious, like a house, but useful."

"Okay, you guys," Lupe said. "Sometimes you get out of control."

"Okay," Maciej said. "Enough, enough. Lupe, what are you and Staś reading these days?"

"We're reading Conrad's *Prince Roman* out loud to each other," Lupe said. "And also we're reading *Pan Tadeusz*. Staś is reading it to me in Polish and English, because last year I read *Don Quixote* to him in Spanish and English."

"We concentrate on the picaresque and the idyllic," Staś said, laughing.

"Yes," Lupe continued, "we're reading the part in *Pan Tadeusz,* the spring of 1812, when everyone is uneasy. The oxen seem to hesitate in the fields when plowing, the country people look with alarm at the sky and wonder at the early return of the migrating birds. Suddenly the cavalry appears out of a cloud of dust. It's something! Staś is translating all this for me; and in *Prince Roman,* the very same scene occurs. The cavalry appears in the distance, like a dragon, flashing steel, making its way across the countryside."

"Ah, *Prince Roman,*" Maciej said. "I remember it so well, that shy little boy, who puts his inky hand into the prince's wrinkled old hand. And at the end of the story, he's across the room from the prince and his father. What a room."

"That's right," Lupe said, "it's the spaces, the rooms, in Conrad. He does them so beautifully."

"And you two look so beautiful tonight," Maciej said.

Lupe laughed, and shook her black hair. "You know, Maciej," she said, "I made Staś a poem. 'Roses are red, violets are blue, daisies are white, and so are you.' He's my *bolillo,* my white roll, my sort of *gringo.*"

51

"Look," Staś said, "now I remember. I have something to show you two. Where's the flashlight?"

Lupe, Maciej, and one of the cats followed Staś out into the night. The porch door slammed behind them. The January wind marched across the Texas night, and yet there was the smell of spring in the air. The trees swayed. Lupe followed Staś, with Maciej and the cat behind, through the dark, around the corner to the south side of the house. Staś turned on the flashlight, and there in the small circle of light, Lupe saw a clump of yellow daffodils half opening into the night.

STAŚ

INTIMATIONS

A woman friend had written to Staś about his complicated erotic life: "Staś, you have so many hats on, it's a wonder you can walk through a door." Staś thought to himself, "I wonder, how many hats could I balance on my penis?" It was true, in his life he had had many affairs, but lately he wanted to be completely faithful to Lupe. Nevertheless he asked Maciej, "How many hats could you carry on your penis?"

"Oh, five or six," Maciej replied. Each began to discuss the hats.

"A fedora, a cap with a woven back like they wear down here, a bowler, a Panama, and on the end, or top, a black stovepipe hat like Lincoln's," Staś said. They were tossing a baseball back and forth across Staś's backyard. The pecan leaves were moist beneath their feet.

"Do you remember that summer we were both living in Warsaw on Grażyna Street?" Staś asked. "We were both so young, twenty-one or twenty-two, and you were having an affair with my cousin Jadwiga. Tell me again how it happened with you and Jadwiga. And watch out for my little garden. Please don't step on my onions."

"Here's how it was," Maciej said. "You know that Witek, her husband, was very brutal. He punched her in the nose. She was black and blue. She went to stay at her aunt's house. She was going to the university, and I met her there. A group of us went dancing, and Jadwiga and I were having a fine time. We danced so well, we were laughing. I asked her to come home with me. I saw that for a minute she hesitated, thinking about her husband and her children, then she laughed and said yes. You know that small apartment my sister had? It was dark when we got home, we had to tiptoe past my sister and her husband sleeping in the kitchen, and we went into my tiny bedroom, barely big enough to hold my single bed."

Staś said, "You know, Jadwiga looks like Gosia."

"Well, you're right," Maciej said.

"Tell me, Maciej, do you think Lupe is having an affair with Vassily?"

"They care for each other, I'm sure," Maciej said, "but you and Lupe are destined for each other."

"Ah, you're such a friend, you have such a feeling for Lupe and me together. You're our archivist," Staś said. "But Maciej, lately I've had such a feeling of mortality. Listen, sometimes I hear these sentences, as if it's the ending of a book:

'In the spring of 1993 Staś died. He had made a lot of money on the stock market, and he left Lupe a wealthy woman. Lupe married Vassily. Vassily admitted to Maciej

and Lupe that he had had an affair with
Gosia for many years. Maciej and his wife
settled in the U.S., and became citizens, and
bought a house in Bandera. Gosia lived
on.' "

"But how did you die?" Maciej asked.

"Well, all of us exiles continue to know each other, and
find it really hard to talk with anyone else. One day, that
spring day in 1993, we decide to go on a picnic, Vassily,
Lupe, you and me. This is a special picnic. We boil lobsters
in advance, cool them, pack them up; Vassily makes that
mayonnaise he makes, and we have plenty of chilled cham-
pagne. We're up in the hill country. We stop by a little
arroyo. What a good lunch we have! But then the car won't
start. I get under the front to take a look. I ask Vassily to
start it up. But I've left the car in first. Nobody notices.
When Vassily starts the car, it leaps forward and crushes my
chest."

"Horrible," Maciej said.

"Tell Lupe I loved her, I've never been so happy with
anyone."

"I will," Maciej said, "and I'll visit Gosia for you."

"I know you will," Staś said. "I always count on you.
And read with Gosia. She loves the part about the rabbits
and their soft fur in *Pan Tadeusz,* that's her favorite part. She
doesn't like Szymborska, or Różewicz, but she very much
enjoys Miłosz, particularly the 'naive' poems. I guess all
American poetry is naive poetry."

"I think Polish poetry can't be naive, ever again,"
Maciej said. "I miss that lyricism."

"I want you to drink deeply at the wedding—Lupe and
Vassily's wedding."

"Oh, I will," Maciej said, "and I'll plant an onion garden like this one here in your memory. What do you plant here?"

"Well, look," Staś explained, "there's chives, evergreen bunching scallions, Bermuda onions, the golden that keeps so well. And we have a few herbs about."

"For certain, some flowers too," Maciej said.

THE DAILY
ROUND

Usually Staś lay in bed stretching and dozing until nine, when he got up and called his broker for a few quotes. Then he fed the cats and drove over to Boerne for breakfast. But this morning he went to the university with Lupe because he wanted to look for Maciej. Maciej had been waiting for some weeks to hear about a research grant. If the grant didn't come through, the university planned to enroll him as a student, so that he could stay another year in the U.S. After Staś dropped off Lupe, he drove by the recreation center where he and Maciej shot baskets in the evenings. Maciej was trying to learn to be American. Ever since Maciej had arrived from Poland, he had worn bluejeans every day, and insisted on playing every sport at the university. When they shot baskets, Maciej and Staś rarely spoke, leaping and falling away from the backboard in silence. When they fished together, they could sit without a word for hours in the boat out on the lake, reeling in the crappies and bass.

As Staś walked toward the biology lab, he passed the batting range where he and Maciej cracked the baseball sharply on spring evenings. The university was a cornucopia of sports for the two friends. Next Staś passed the aquatic center where he liked to swim slowly on rainy days. When Staś arrived at the lab, he found that Maciej had left on a trip to Austin, so he drove back along the interstate to Boerne, and parked in front of the diner. Today the town was as empty as the moon. Staś let himself in the door by the Smart 'n Thrifty Shop, and walked upstairs to his studio. Halfway up the stairs, he began to meow, just to entertain himself. By the time he reached the top of the stairs he was cackling like an offended hen. Diffuse light streamed in through the windows. In the morning light all the paintings on the walls looked beautiful; like embarkations for Cythera. Vast golden surfaces. Each painting was at least ten or eleven feet long, and about six feet high. Barking angrily, Staś mixed up the colors he would use for the day and settled into his work. Time passed, and after a few hours he began to caw like a crow at daybreak. He cleaned up, tinkered for a while with a floor polisher with which he was planning to try painting. He would have to get a new disk fabricated for the head of the machine.

Staś went downstairs and walked across the broad street to have lunch. He was making a study of what people said as they rose from their tables to leave. At the moment of rising, they talked louder, as if addressing the whole lunchroom.

Today two women got up, and the younger said to the older, "They haven't been married very long. She doesn't know if she's happy or not." Staś held his hands up parenthetically, trying to picture the happiness held between his two hands. A minute later a man leaned forward to get up, and said to the two women who had eaten with him, "Lipstick on coffee cups, it's as American as apple pie."

Staś walked back to his studio and worked on some pencil drawings until almost three, when he drove over to a brokerage house in San Antonio to catch the closing of the New York Exchange. He always stood behind the old guys, who sat in leather chairs gazing up at the Teletrade board. One of Staś's stocks was up two points. Suddenly he felt happy, just for a moment, before he started to wonder again about the nature of happiness. He walked to the car and drove to the library at the university where he read the papers and studied the previous day's closing stock quotes. Lupe met him at five, and they decided to drive back into San Antonio for dinner.

"This car is always messy," Staś exclaimed, as he got into the car. Lupe looked startled.

"Messy, it's only my jacket. What about the magazines in your car?"

"I'm going to take those magazines to my studio," Staś said. "Then, when people go up there and see the *TLS, Tygodnik Nowojorski, The Economist,* and *The Daily Investor,* they will know exactly what kind of person I am."

"Mmmhmm," Lupe said. "I know you just take that *Tygodnik Nowojorski* up there to look at the woman of the week. Who was that one in white gloves and stockings, the one who worked for the plastic surgeon?"

"Mmmhmm," Staś said. "She was beautiful, but not as beautiful as you."

"Sure. And aren't you going to see Gosia when you go to Houston tomorrow?"

"Oh Lupe, she doesn't mean anything to me anymore. I sent her some slides of my new paintings, and I just want to stop by and hear what she thinks, on the way to see the lawyer about our tax forms. Believe me."

"Mmmhmm," Lupe said.

"Hey, what's it look like?" Staś asked.

"Like rain, Staś. I thought I heard thunder."

"Here, turn here," Staś said. "Let's go to Red Lobster, and eat those little crayfish or lobsters or whatever they are."

During dinner, Staś recounted the stock events of the week. By buying Merrill Lynch at 36 and selling at 38, buying again at 37 and selling at 39¼, they had made $4,250. "Not bad, let's see, that would be $200,000 a year if I did so well every week. The Financial News Network is already up to 9. All the stocks are in perfect position, except for those problematical options I just bought."

Just then a voice from the next booth said, "Yeah, but the market's going to fall to 1,400."

"Huh?" Staś said. He looked up and saw an ugly redheaded guy.

"Yeah, the L.A. Wave Analyst says the Dow is going down to 1,400."

"No, it's not," Staś said, "it's going up until April, I've just got a hunch about it." Staś felt irritated at the intrusion. He talked in a quieter voice to Lupe.

"Cross yourself," Lupe said, "or make the sign against the *ojo* under the table."

When they got home, Lupe lay down on the bed, her legs hanging over the side. Staś stood over her, his legs touching hers. He began to snake back and forth from side to side. Lupe laughed. He bent and slid his chest slowly up her body, from her thighs to her waist to her shoulders. Now he lay lightly on her.

"Do you want to?" he asked.

"I do."

SEPARATION

The next day Staś and Lupe stayed in bed late. On the way to the airport, Staś went over with Lupe all that he had to do in Houston. He didn't mention the real reason for the trip, that there was something he still had to resolve with Gosia, and that he wanted to read Gosia a certain poem. Instead Staś described how he would work on their taxes with their lawyer, take some drawings to the framer, see his analyst, and speak briefly with Gosia about his paintings and his hopes that she might exhibit his work. But this seemed boring compared to the wonderful stories Lupe began to tell him about life in the small Mexican town where she grew up. He listened raptly for half an hour, then said, "But we must go there. Or you must go back, even without me. Why not this summer?" Would he fit into such a town, he wondered? Wouldn't it be easier for Lupe to be alone with her relatives?

He kissed her goodbye at the airport, and watched as she drove away. Then he went inside and got some newspapers, and lounged around at the breakfast bar before he went to get his seat assignment, and to board the plane.

The plane was old. It rattled and shook as it built up speed, and didn't seem to lift off properly. Staś crossed himself. Once the plane was airborne, it quickly passed from the obscuring fog below the clouds into the clear blue air above. It was a short trip, fifty minutes to Houston. Staś looked down with wonder at the clouds, which were arranged this morning in faultless parallel furrows, extending from below the plane to far away at the horizon, in perfect order, wave after wave. Staś reflected that this was very different from the usual sheepswool, random, tufted pattern that he saw on overcast days. He suddenly noticed, beneath the plane, a halo of prismatic colors that traveled over the clouds at the same rate as the plane. The halo's colors were arranged like a rainbow, with the yellow on the inside, the indigo and violet on the outside, and within the halo appeared the small, perfectly distinct shadow of the airplane making its way through the sky. Staś grasped for the word for this—a "glory," that's what it was; a circular rainbow was called a "glory." The plane began to slow and sink towards Houston. The "glory" and the shadow grew larger, blurrier, approaching rapidly, becoming as large as the plane itself, and at that moment the plane plunged through its own shadow, and plummeted downward through the clouds. Staś held his breath in amazement. This is certainly an experience one can't have on earth, Staś thought. On earth one can't plunge through, or penetrate, one's own shadow. And disappear.

He felt elated and hardly noticed the long delay in deplaning. That night he called Lupe and described his amazing experience to her.

"Staś, you know I love you," she said.

"I love you too," he said." I'll go to the gallery tomorrow. I'll see you soon."

Staś put on a dark suit and tie. In the mirror he looked like a wintry Holbein portrait. He had read somewhere that if you shaved your beard downward, rather than upward, the next day you would have the sort of stubble that women found so attractive these days. Today, this stubble articulated his cheeks and jawbone like the lines of trees on a distant snowy mountain. He looked gaunt, serious and sad. He put on his long black coat, and a somber black hat, and went out into the sunshine.

Staś went to his bank, and gave the teller the key, and she brought him his safety deposit box. He took it into one of the small rooms the bank provided for its customers. He made a list of all the gold certificates in the box. Then he lifted a packet of letters out of the box and, feeling for the envelope that was thickest, opened it and removed three black-and-white photographs. The first photo he had taken of Gosia years ago at the Łazienki Palace. She wore a tweed coat and black gloves, and stood beside the wall looking shy and wild, almost startled. The next was of an older Gosia, in a spotted summer dress, sitting in a deck chair on somebody's yacht. And the last photo was rather recent, of Gosia at a party. She was turned towards the camera, looking with surprise, eyebrows raised, at whomever had snapped the photo. Staś put his head into his hands.

Back on the street he checked to make sure he had the copy of Gérard de Nerval's poems with him. He had brought this book to read the poem on melancholy to Gosia. It was an old joke. She had always found Gérard de

Nerval and Staś ridiculously melodramatic in their melancholy.

When he arrived at the gallery, he was reluctant to go inside. He walked around outdoors for a long time. A sign on the window said, "Watercolors by Maud." Finally he walked in.

The gallery was a long rectangular space with blond waxed floors. Gosia sat at the front desk. She looked up at Staś, and said, "Darling."

"Who is that person?" Staś asked, pointing to the framed pieces hung on the wall.

"She's an Irishwoman," Gosia said. "Maud. She's in love with me."

A ridiculous pronouncement, Staś thought to himself. Preposterous.

"Come right into the office, I want to show you the spring schedule."

Staś felt irritated, and remembered suddenly how Gosia and he always seemed to want to talk to each other at the same time. He followed her into the office, and put the Gérard de Nerval book on her desk.

"But you look so gloomy," Gosia said.

"I thought I looked well in black."

"No, I think gray for you." She tugged his necktie, and rearranged it. "Here, look at this schedule. Lupe's show is next."

He read the schedule on the table. After Lupe's show, there would be Twentieth-Century European Masters, then some hot young Post-Expressionists from New York, followed by a show of ceramics by local Mexican-American artists. "I want to do a show of skeleton figures, Day of the Dead items, and costumes, in the fall," Gosia said.

"Yes," Staś said.

"I think I'll call it 'The Ancestors.' "

"Well, that sounds good."

"But you seem out of sorts. I want to talk to you about your paintings. Here, sit down."

He sat and looked at her. What a handsome woman she is, he thought. Her dress was worked with a gold and green pattern that seemed to slide like water around her: a woman to swim in, he thought. The slash of lipstick was so thick on her lips that he could see fissures in it. The older a woman gets, the more lipstick she wears, he decided.

"I received your slides," Gosia said.

"And what did you think?"

"Your paintings just go on and on. They don't seem to make any sense. They lack closure. Staś, your paintings don't have any boundaries."

"I don't have any boundaries," Staś said.

"You mean you fill all earth and space?" Gosia teased.

"Well, yes," Staś said. He thought for a minute. "The lack of boundary, the apparent aimlessness, is actually a tactic, a motive. I want my paintings to look totally without presumption, to flow without pomposity, like a river without end, on which events pass simply and serenely."

"I can't sell these, Staś."

"Does it matter? All I care about is nakedness, simplicity. I want a painting to be absolutely naked, like that Goya drawing of a man we saw in New York. Remember when we went to that collector's house—what's the name of the drawing? Not *El Desdichado* but—"

"I know which one you mean," Gosia said.

"Yes, like that, the subtle variations in tone, and all made of nothing."

"Staś, I wish I could help you, but I can't, at least not right now."

Staś felt a pain in his chest, but he said, "I don't even care, really. I paint for myself, and not for the world."

"Why don't you come over tonight? My ex just flew in, and we'll have a jolly time."

Staś instantly envisioned too much vodka, too much marijuana, a night that would certainly end in stupor, with Gosia's boorish ex-husband asleep on the couch or on the floor. He still wanted to make love with Gosia, but in another time, before they had both learned so much about the world and how to survive in it. "No thanks, darling," he said sadly, "I want to go to bed early and read. I have to get up early too, to do some business."

"Oh, come on, Staś," Gosia teased. "After he falls asleep, you can come to my room, like the old days."

"Really, I can't."

"Then call me tomorrow."

"*Kochanie,* darling, I will."

"*Ukochany,* dear Staś," Gosia said. She kissed him. He lingered for a moment and put up his hand to stroke her silver-black hair. Then he walked through the gallery and out to the street. That night he realized he had left his book on her table. He went down to the hotel bar to get a drink. He sat at the dark counter. Two women were talking next to him. "That's how I got my condo," one woman said.

"How?" the woman on the further barstool asked.

"Watching jockeys. Now you take a certain jockey, well I won't say who, he's got a horse in the number eight-nine-ten-eleven position, and he comes out of the gate and crosses over too soon. The horse quits right after. Or, you can watch the field. A big field, more money is bet. I like a big Derby with two starting gates. I got a guy gives me the right horse every time."

"But how does the size of the field affect such a thing?" Staś asked without hesitation.

"Well hello, honey," the woman said, turning around. In the light of the bar Staś saw that she had bright red hair. The word "tacky" instantly crossed his mind, and then the word "hot."

"But I'm serious, what happens when there are more horses?" Staś asked.

"More money bet, sweetie, and your favorite is more likely to win, oddly enough, in some cases." The woman smiled at Staś.

Staś felt physically hot. This is how it begins, he thought. Destinies cross. This redhead and I could end up in bed. The prospect excited and repelled him. He felt weary of his infidelities, and decided not to go on with it any further. "Look darlings," he said, "Let me give you a tip on stocks."

"Oh yeah," the other woman said.

"Yes," Staś said, "Compaq options. Just keep buying and selling calls." It was strange how a conversation could be turned so easily, he thought.

When he got back to the room he called Lupe. "It's the same as always, she doesn't think she can sell my paintings."

"Staś, you knew she'd say that. You're a genius, you can't expect to be understood."

"Ah, that's right," Staś said, "I always forget."

THE RETURN

Staś cracked open the *Wall Street Journal*. The plane was almost empty on the journey back. The windows were dark. He traced the columns. Here it was, Dart & Kraft, his first love. This was the first stock that had ever made him money. And now, in a week's time, it had risen from 45 to 52. Already he had made $7,000 on it, and it had reached a new high. Staś felt unusually content. His analyst had told him, "Maybe, although it was a sad thing to bring your affair with Gosia to an end, you will be a more whole person. Your many affairs with women, your double life with your wife and lovers, were a way of 'fucking' women. Making love in airplanes, one night stands in hotel rooms, it's as if you don't care for anyone." But could a person really change? Staś wondered. Could one's life change as simply as picking up a new book? Did another life stretch out before him, one in which he might be a substantially different person, almost a stranger to himself? Would he possibly even die happily? Die a happy man?

The plane landed in San Antonio. Staś came off the airplane fourth in line, and walked down the ramp to the lounge. Lupe was waiting. "Staszek," she said, "You look so thin."

"Lupita."

They laughed, and Lupe started to cry. They began to walk towards the exit.

"You're glad to see me," Staś exclaimed.

"Oh yes, I am, Staś."

"Usually we both laugh," Staś said.

"I know, but I worried about you. You're so thin, and why are you so unshaved?"

"Oh well, I thought it was fashionable, to bristle like this. And I didn't feel well yesterday, I couldn't eat."

"Well you must shave before you get into bed, and I have a surprise for you. It's too late to drive home, it's already 11:30, I got a room for us at that motel. I was already there, watching a special on this woman who carved every figure in the Bible in miniature. She had to keep adding rooms to her house."

"Hmm, sounds interesting," Staś said. He hugged her as they reached the exit, and paused. The black glass doors slid open, and then closed behind them as they walked out into the night.

The next day, after work at the studio, Staś drove to the botanical garden. He wanted to spend time with the Himalayan pine, the Tibetan fir, and all the other "visiting trees," as he thought of them. He walked down the slope to the exotic-tree section, and nodded with satisfaction at the beauty of the pine, whose branches looked like mares' tails lifted up, blowing in the wind, like a drawing in wash. He walked further downhill to a tree Lupe and he always called 'Maciej,' because it seemed to resemble their friend so perfectly. It was a winged elm, about fifteen feet high, with thick corky flanges running up either side of each limb. This too reminded Staś of the Orient, the flanges seemed like those of ancient bronze vessels. There was something so reserved, ancient, timeless about this tree. It was a throwback to the past, like the horsetail, the gingko. The trees seemed to vex Staś into thought. He felt as if he had lived forever, known these trees forever. He walked back up the hill and drove home.

He parked the sports car behind the house and climbed out, remembering that he wanted to wash the car by the back faucet. Suddenly he heard a high shrill sound coming from high up in the trees. He looked up and saw hundreds of cedar waxwings in the pecan tree above him, in fact in all the trees. The thin sound seemed to lift him up by the ears into the trees. He felt like one of the small birds himself, sitting on a limb. Staś watched and listened, until group after group of the little birds began to fly off, flashing the thin yellow stripe on their tails.

Staś went indoors and called Lupe at the art department office. He knew she would be typing there from two o'clock till five.

"Art office," she said.

"Ah Lupe," Staś said, "there were hundreds of waxwings here."

"¡Ay!, but Staś," Lupe said, "they were just here an hour ago. We were watching them outside, and I thought of you. What a sound, they were going, 'Eeeeeeeee.' "

"But isn't that something," Staś said. "They flew from you to me. But what's the name for this? A poetic fallacy? Pathetic fallacy? What's that expression for when nature appears to be in sympathy?"

"I don't know, Staszek. But what are you doing?"

"Well, I'm going to wash the sports car and listen to the financial news."

"That's good. Don't sell any stocks. I'll be home at six to cook supper," Lupe said.

POTWÓR

But the next day Staś didn't feel so content, and he doubted that he could live up to his plan to be faithful. How simple it had all appeared yesterday. Overnight he had dreamed of Gosia. In the dream, Gosia stood some distance from him in a crowded room, talking animatedly with an old guy. "Excuse me," he dreamed he heard Gosia say, "I have to go ingratiate myself with that old so and so." He remembered Gosia telling him this once at a party. He watched her gesturing as she emphasized some point, turning her head this way and that in a compelling manner. Abruptly she noticed Staś, and left the old guy and came over to him. "I haven't been able to forget you," she said. "The way we courted and loved each other was so beautiful. Dance with me." They began to dance slowly and elegantly around the room, in the manner and style of another century. Staś noticed that he was stroking her back in a rhythmic, sexual way, and at the same moment he realized that Gosia's hand had slipped below his belt to his trousers. Staś awoke with a cry. He lay in bed shocked, letting the excitement subside. Happiness now seemed to him to reside in only one circumstance: the reclaiming of a past instance. No matter what the past was, it always appeared lovelier than the present. Wasn't he the most at ease, wasn't his life fullest, during that summer he had spent in Warsaw with Maciej and Jadwiga when he was twenty-six? Even when they were very poor, his cousin Jadwiga had kept a little dog. Potwór, his name was— Monster. Staś used to lie on the apartment floor and play with Potwór. He was a black, wiry scamp, a very clever dog who would lift his paw up and put it against you, and look into your eyes with such a deep look. And he was so free. He was the very essence of freedom. In fact, Potwór seemed to Staś to be very like himself, insistent on freedom, even on license. And a man is a little bit of a dog in his moments of greatest happiness, Staś thought, especially a dog when he's hunting for something like a bone, or a lovely female. "But I'm a dog," Staś said out loud, startling himself. He sat up in bed because he suddenly remembered that he had promised to pick up the truck from Lupe's parents, so that Lupe could use it to drive her paintings to Houston.

LUPE

THE PHONE
CALL
FROM VASSILY

They were in the kitchen. Lupe's kitchen was pewter gray, the ceiling light blue. Staś's contribution to the kitchen was a prism that turned slowly on a thread, high in the window. Lupe had hung small delicate brooms of various sorts and shapes on the walls. It was evening. Lupe was heating tortillas over the gas stove, and Staś sat at the table cutting onions. The phone rang. Lupe moved from the stove to the phone.

"Hello," she said.

"Hello you little witch. I know Staś is sitting around and you're cooking for him. He doesn't deserve you."

"Vassily, where are you?" Lupe demanded.

"Sweetheart, that's not important, let's just say that I'm calling from a cloud. I want to ask you a favor. But first how are you?"

"Oh we're fine," Lupe said, "Staś is actually doing a

little work, now he's cutting the avocado. Staś, do you want to talk with Vassily?"

"No, just say hello."

"You see Vassily, he's such a *huevón,* he can't even get off his big balls to come to the phone."

"Tell him I'm going fishing with Maciej," Staś said. "Why doesn't he come to the ranch, and we'll show him our country pleasures?"

"He's on a cloud dear, he doesn't have time. Right?" Lupe said, resuming her conversation with Vassily. "What is it you need?"

"That kind of Mexican, very sweet candy I love so much, *tú sabes?* It looks like fruit, like you, dearest. Could you pick me up some and leave it with Gosia when you go to Houston?"

"*Sí,*" Lupe said, trying to steady her voice.

"Many thanks. And you'll give my love to all, to your family, your father, your mother, and Faustino in Monterrey?"

"But how do you remember his name?"

"But my dear, I hold all your relatives in my heart."

"*¡Ay!,* Vassily, we've missed you. *¿ Y por qué no vienes a visitarnos?* We always enjoy your visit."

"Soon, soon sweetheart. But I must go. *Besos, abrazos, amor.*"

Lupe brought the tortillas to Staś. She sat down at the table, and as they ate she listened through the screen to the noises of the night.

THE POSTCARD

Lupe was in a nagging mood the next morning. "You still didn't get the truck, and now we'll have to wake up my parents on Saturday, that's my father's day off."

"I'll get it later today," Staś said.

"No, I'll go change cars. I want to go to the Botica, you know that one down on South Flores Street."

"Alright," Staś said. "I'll come in later. I want to stay in bed and think a while."

Lupe took the Buick and drove into town. Nobody was at home at her parents' house, so she left the keys to the Buick on the kitchen table and took the truck. Lupe liked being alone in the truck. She felt very content, as she drove along in a style she had seen on TV, not grasping the wheel with her fingers, but splaying her right hand out, touching the wheel with only her small palm. The ease of the power steering allowed her to turn the truck in this manner, describing circles left and right with her outstretched hand.

And why not? Lupe thought. Driving like this is very *Pachuco* and American at the same time. With such things on her mind, she almost drove by the candymaker's. She parked the truck, and went into the store. The fruit candies were displayed in cardboard boxes under the counter. She chose a banana, a pomegranate and an orange. The dull sticky colors were so familiar to her. Ever since she was a child her father had brought these candies home to the family. The red reminded her of something else. The dull red, the thickness of the dull red, was almost like leather. That's what it was: the sandals that Gosia had worn the last time she had seen her and they had talked about the installation of Lupe's show. "Yes, you'll come to Houston early, and we'll hang the show a few days in advance," Gosia had said. And Lupe had noticed how large Gosia's feet were, how Gosia's feet seemed to be crammed into the thick red sandals she was wearing. But why was she thinking about Gosia's feet? She decided that she had better send Gosia a postcard. After all, wasn't this what white people did, send cards? She paid for the fruit, and watched the man at the counter tie the package with string. Then she put the package under her arm and walked across the street to the postcard store. On the rack she saw a scene that she at once recognized—a playground for children in Monterrey where she herself had been when she was little. She decided to send this card to Gosia. The gate to the playground was a monstrous mouth, which seemed to devour the children as they passed down the steps into the throat. Beyond the mouth one could see children on the swings and the slide. Lupe bought the card and took out her pen. Her hand trembled as she wrote. This big white woman Gosia always made her feel a little breathless, as if she had just been running around the track at the university and suddenly had to stop to talk to someone. *Poder,* Lupe thought: Perhaps it is her power. She has a power.

Lupe finished the card and walked up the street to the Botica. The girls at the counter were talking about a popular singer. She selected a certain type of crystalline rock she needed for curing, and several diminutive brooms for *la limpia,* the sweeping away of illness or of *susto,* the sudden fright that Staś sometimes experienced. At those times she had to give him a spoonful of honey, and sweep his body with one of the little brooms. How much he loved her after this. He was as quiet as a small child when she took care of him.

"Where can I mail this card?" she asked the salesgirl.

"We'll mail it for you," the girl said.

"No, I'd better mail it," Lupe decided. She drove back to her parents' house, and put the card in the mailbox out on the street. Inside the house she found Staś and Concepción sitting in the front room staring at the TV from a distance of two feet. "Shhh," Staś said, "it's an old movie; Lucha Villa is in it. We're waiting for Lucha Villa to appear."

PARTING

The next day they had to pack the paintings in the truck. On their way to the university they passed a flea market. Two small children sat in front of the market with big buckets of gladioli. Staś drove on. Lupe cried, "Stop, stop, we must go back and get some, they're white."

"Who, the children?" Staś asked.

"No, the gladioli," Lupe said. They drove back. Staś bought a dozen white gladioli.

"How could there be gladioli at this time of year?" Staś asked.

"I don't know. Perhaps they're from the valley, or from some other country," Lupe said. "Look how beautiful they are." She held them across her lap.

At the university they brought the paintings down in the elevator. Staś had made cardboard sleeves to protect the edges and corners. He slipped the cardboard pieces onto the paintings, which Lupe had already wrapped in plastic. Lupe fitted them neatly into the truck.

"You don't mind that you're not coming to the show?"

"No, really, not at all."

"It's just that I don't want to be thought of as the Polish émigré speculator's lovely Mexican wife Lupe, ¿ tú sabes?"

"But I understand perfectly. You'll have such a good time," Staś said. "And it's interesting, I feel quite abstract, totally unanchored, when you're not here. Perhaps I'll write a book; I've been thinking about a book I'd like to write, *That Other Medicine: The Curandero.* That's what I'd call it, what do you think?"

"What do you know about it?"

"Well, everything that you and Concepción do."

"It's better not to write about it."

"Then I'll talk with Babka. I'll get Maciej to bring Babka over. He's going to be in Dallas anyway to meet his wife. They're going to have a second honeymoon for a week or two."

They drove home from the university. Lupe arranged the gladioli blooms, spreading them out in a fan shape before the kitchen window in a white vase. The effect was dazzling in the afternoon sunshine. "It's the white," Lupe said. "I must grow white flowers some year."

STAŚ

THE
HAMMOCK

Early the next morning Lupe left for Houston. Staś sat and looked at the gladioli arranged in the kitchen window. Then he went outdoors to work on the property. He raked up the live oak leaves in the driveway and the yard. When he put away the rake, he found a little hawk lying dead on the ground under the window of the barn. He picked up the hawk and examined its long barred wings, its rufous back, the curved yellow claws, the distinguished black moustache marks against the white on either side of the sharply curved beak. Staś didn't want to draw the bird, as he might have earlier in his life. He laid the hawk under the prickly pears by the side of the fence. When he drew something like this nowadays, he felt it distanced him from life. He wanted to be the bird, rather than to study the bird.

He decided next to take the sheets of plastic off the

north windows. He wanted to let fresh air into the house. He had many things to do before Lupe returned, but today the work didn't go smoothly. One of the slats of wood that held the plastic down sailed through the air when Staś tugged on the plastic, and hit him on the head. He shrugged, as if to say, perhaps this was not the day for this, and walked through the tall weeds to the hammock. Before climbing into the hammock, he removed a matchbox from the inside pocket of his jacket, and opened it. He looked at the earth he had put in there last fall. He sprinkled the dry powder from the matchbox out onto the ground, and put a fresh daub of earth into the box. The dirt cohered to itself. Soon it would crack and dry. He would carry the dust of their property next to his heart.

He swung one leg up into the hammock, and then the other, and presto, he was airborne. He sank back into the hammock and, pulling on a branch, started the hammock swaying. The river ran in bright bars of blue light and black shadow only a few steps from where he swung. He looked directly up through the branches, and then back at the river, whose fluid brightness approached and passed him. What can we make of this? he thought. He felt gently hypnotized by the flickering light, and fell asleep, remembering the time his uncle Andrzej had stood on the back porch in Maryland and had called to an owl, and the owl had called back and flown from the dark spruce trees to land on his uncle's shoulder. Staś too had communion with birds. Sometimes, as he swung in this hammock, a sparrow would land on his toe or knee, and as long as Staś swung, the sparrow would take no notice of where it was perched. But as soon as the hammock stopped, the startled bird would take off in a hurry.

Staś woke up with a start. He had dreamed of communion wafers dipped in some substance that he did not recognize. In the dream, he ate two wafers, tipped his head back, and experienced two jolts of unbelievably absorbing pleasure.

Staś sat up in the hammock. Wasn't he, Staś, like the snail Maciej had brought him from a trip to Greece? Everyone had admired the handsome shell on the mantelpiece and then one day, when the creature inside curiously stuck forth its gray-brown head and pseudopodic antennae, everyone had been startled and wondered how to nourish the creature.

Were art and money enough? Was it enough to paint, draw, to do a few kind acts, to love one's friends, to love one's wife, to love the earth, to have lost consciousness in a woman's arms? Had he understood anything at all? He climbed out of the hammock and walked into the house. He sat down at the kitchen table and worked at figures, lightly pressing the digits of the calculator with his finger as he added up the week's gains. The 100,000 shares of NOVA Pharmaceutical had made him $30,000 in one week. Why did he enjoy speculating, and only a few other things in life? Would he ever understand all of being; would he ever enter into harmony with being and meld into the air? He lit the gas jet on the stove to make some tea, and the pleasant smell of tortillas rose from the burner. The phone rang. A woman friend from several years back wanted to sell him a car he had once admired.

"Remember, the El Camino, 1959, 283 engine, 3 speeds on the column? For you, only $4,000." Staś remembered the car. It was a beauty. But he and Lupe already had three cars. He was always spending money fixing them, reshaping their rusty fenders with Bondo, trying to make them last forever.

"I don't know," he said to the woman, "I'll have to talk with Lupe, we already have three cars. But thanks for calling."

"Want to come over and have a drink?"

Staś remembered meeting the woman in an airport, making love with her in a shower in a summer house.

"No, I can't, I'm going out of town," he lied. "But I'll call soon, I promise. I'll call you about the car." He hung up.

Doesn't death lurk in cars? he thought. In more ways than one. Maybe he should sell all the cars, and then the only thing he would know of rust was the rusty color of that bird, the red brown sparrow hawk.

BY TELEPHONE
i

That night Lupe called. "I'm here at my sister's house," she said.

"Ah, thank goodness you're safe," Staś said. "Listen Lupe, you know that woman in Alamo Heights who has the '59 El Camino? She wants to sell it."

"Buy it, Staszek."

"Buy it? You seem to be in such a good mood. I thought you'd say no."

"No, we must have that car. It's the first car I remember from my childhood. My father had one. We can keep it in the barn."

"But the barn is smaller than the car. This car is something like twenty-two feet long."

"Buy it Staś, we'll never regret it. We can put a tarp

over the part that sticks out. All Mexicans do this, and nobody will touch it. My mother will love it."

"Alright, I'll send a down payment. Listen Lupe, do you have time to hear a story?"

"Yes. But first I want to know. What else did that woman try to sell you? Her bed? Did she try to seduce you on the phone? I remember that witch."

"No, really, it was just business."

"I'm sure Staszek. I hope you feel guilty."

"I do, sweetheart."

"Now you can tell me the story."

"I mean I feel guilty even though nothing happened."

"Just feel guilty the whole time I'm away," Lupe said. "Now what is the story?"

"I walked out after supper. I went up the river and lay by a boulder. I fell asleep, or was entranced, many minutes. When I awoke everything seemed removed from me: money, cars, gambling."

"Mmmhmm."

"Shall I go on?"

"Of course."

"Then I thought that all of learning is like sand being put through a series of finer and finer sieves, till finally there's little left. But the point is not that little rarefied amount that's left, but that something big has been removed. Something big got knocked out at the very beginning. Now when I paint or draw, I spread a net, as anyone does. Some spread a fine net—I do too—but I leave a hole in the net through which either a big fish has already escaped, or through which a big fish will or can escape. This hole is a blank spot on a canvas, an erasure in a drawing, an opening that confounds everything, through which the fish can slip. I know I know nothing. Leaving the hole is admitting that the fish exists. My genius or contribution will come from finding something totally out of the blue, new under the sun. If I fail, at least I left the blank space for it to have happened. At least I sensed it. It's like looking at a river for many years. You think you know it. Then one day a cat with fur swims by under the surface of the water. Your hair stands on end. The cat climbs out of the water and slithers into a hole in the bank. It's a muskrat. You've never seen a muskrat before. It confounds everything you know. There's something out there nobody knows. It's the opposite of redesigning the elements on a building to change it from Gothic to Renaissance. You know how the facade of Santa Maria Novella is nothing but a Gothic facade redone by Alberti. So it is with all thinkers, they're readjusting this idea and that, but there's something that leaving a hole in the net acknowledges—something we know nothing about. Sometimes I feel it swim by me, I feel the stir of it, but I don't know yet what it is, or if I ever will. But whatever it is, will be—or could have been—my greatness."

"Ah, but Staszek, you're suffering."

"I know Lupe, waiting for this thing is the only thing that makes me go on living. I envision my own demise with satisfaction: I've taken care of everything, you'll have land and cars. And yet I'm curious, I want to stay around for another glimpse. Remember that dark velvety night we walked by the lake, and as we stirred the air, fish leapt out of the water following us as we walked along the bank. Were we stirring mosquitoes? What were they leaping for?"

"Staś, you'll be glad when I get home. Already you're lonely. I think you miss me more than you know."

"¡Ay!, yes I do."

"Look, make Maciej bring Babka over. You're always happy with her. Staś, I've got to go now. I'm having lunch with Gosia. The show opens in three days."

"You must be excited. It will look beautiful. Call me soon."

"Mmm yes," Lupe said. Staś heard her kiss kisses into the phone and hang up.

BY TELEPHONE
ii

The next morning Lupe called again and they talked for a long time. Lupe listened patiently.

"You know, Lupe," Staś said, "the dean in *The Dean's December* is the only guy who's really intelligent in all of American fiction. And the part where he follows his wife up the spiral staircase—was it a spiral staircase? Anyway, the part where he follows her up a spiral into the stars, into the star observatory, is the most beautiful moment in all of American fiction."

"I know, Staś, how much you like that book. I remember you said the dean and his wife were like us, being from two different cultures, communicating, and yet not communicating. Sometimes you seem very Mexican to me, other times, quite from another planet. Well look, Staś, honey, I have to go. Oh wait, can you help me with something? I have to go to dinner at Gosia's house the night before the opening, and her son is going to be there. How do you say his name?"

"Wieńczysław," Staś said. "Just say Wenceslas, like good King Wenceslas."

"He's so pale and delicate," Lupe said.

"His father is fair and slender," Staś said. "It's like Balzac says—wait a minute, I remember the exact words— he speaks of the marriage of feminine force and masculine weakness, a species of contradiction very frequent in Poland. '*Le mariage . . .*' "

"What's this book?" Lupe asked.

"*La Cousine Bette,*" Staś said. "We'll read it together. I know you'll like it."

"I know I will. But Staś, I've really got to go. I was supposed to leave at nine. I'll call you tonight."

BY TELEPHONE
iii

Staś woke from sleep. The phone was ringing. It was almost 2 A.M. He stretched across the bed. "Hello," he said.

"Compadre."

"¡Ay!, querido, Vassily," Staś said. "Where are you?"

"I'm in Ybor City with Dr. Keys."

"Dr. Keys?"

"Dr. Keys is a keyboardist," Vassily explained. "I'm down here in the old city, Ybor, within the city of Tampa, by the docks. I met Dr. Keys, and he wanted me to come down here with him, so here I am. He's not a doctor, but he has, *tú sabes,* in his little black bag, something every woman wants. Why don't you come down here, it's like the old Cuba, very nice."

"I can't come. I'm guarding the fort. Lupe's show opens in two days."

"Yes, I just called Gosia, and then I called Lupe," Vassily explained. "That's how I knew where she was. She says to tell you she'll be coming home soon with fish-net stockings on."

"Then she told you about my idea, about the fish net?"

"Yes, she did, but Staś, she says you keep emphasizing the hole in the net through which the big fish could swim, but that opening in the net is also to provide the fish a place to enter, right?"

"Yes," Staś said, "But it's not important to detain the fish. On the contrary, everything is flux, the stock market, the river. Once in a zoo in Honolulu I heard a familiar sound. It was a robin in a cage. Horrible. Even at Lupe's cousins' house in Monterrey I can't stand the mourning dove in the cage in the courtyard, though it is very beautiful, the gray bird, the white wall."

"You know, Staś, that's something I've been thinking about. How did Lupe get her talent? Maybe it's from her mother. Every room in the house is done in those perfect grays, those off-whites, those strange gray-greens and gray-pinks that Lupe uses.

"I never thought of it," Staś said, "But, of course—how her mother did the kitchen in white and green, it's just like Lupe's palette."

"And speaking of art, how is Gosia?"

"Her ex-husband came from Hong Kong, the one who's in the CIA. I think he's left by now."

"Ah, but this will revive her," Vassily said. "He'll have left her all that high-grade opium and excellent marijuana, and she'll become her reckless old self again."

"Maybe," Staś said.

"Staś, I told you about my new project," Vassily went on. "Maybe I've had enough of the art business. I'm thinking of managing a rock group, The Radon Sisters. I've been busy at it twenty-four hours a day. I've done some sketches for their costumes."

"I'd like to see your sketches very much."

"*Pero compadre,* I'll send them."

"And what else are you doing?"

"Well, I have to be in New York to sell that Braque, and some people are coming over from publishing houses to see about books of my photographs. So I can't be here long, but I want you to come down sometime and meet Dr. Keys. There are many tigresses here, *tipas cubanas, tú sabes.* You'd love it."

"I can't come right now. I'm fixing up the house. But come visit us. We've just bought a '59 El Camino, a monster."

"But this is strange," Vassily said. "I just bought a black '67 Fury with gold stars all over it and I want to take some photos of Lupe in it. Staś, I've got to go. Dr. Keys has just finished playing for the night, and we're going out in a boat. *Adiós.*"

"*Do widzenia,*" Staś said. He got up and closed the window. Then he slipped back into bed and fell asleep.

GOSIA

THE STUDY

L̶iszka stretched out her muzzle as far as she could on her front paws and looked up at Gosia, who read at the table nearby. Liszka was an unprepossessing little dog, tan, with a white stripe on her chest. She was almost useless, helpless as a baby. She was always getting lost, unable even to find her way home from the neighbor's house. Her favorite spot was on her mistress's lap. If not there, she liked to lie curved, beside the fire, just as she did tonight, gazing up at Gosia with her soft worried eyes.

Gosia said, "Ppppuh," as if disagreeing with something she was reading. She closed the book. She took her glasses off. Lately her eyes seemed to bother her. The light from the fire and the reading lamp did not reach out far enough into the reddish-brown darkness gathering in the room. Gosia took a cigarette and lit it.

"This book is Dumesnil's study of *Bouvard et Pécuchet,* which Vassily sent to me," she said. Liszka cocked her ears forward and watched as Gosia took a piece of paper from a pad. Gosia's two green jade bracelets slid down to her wrist and tapped against the table as she wrote on the paper, *"Staś et Vassily, sont-ils des imbéciles?"*

PREPARATIONS

"One is easily cured of a passion for a woman of my age," Gosia said. She was speaking on the bedroom telephone to one of her gallery artists.

"Not so," Maud protested, on the other end of the line.

"You're just being a child," Gosia said. "If I were going to be with a woman, I'd want to be with someone much different from you. I'll tell you what, dear, I'll see you at the gallery tomorrow."

Gosia hung up the phone with a sense of relief. Last year she had met Maud. She had decided to show Maud's work, and they had read some Polish poetry together, but lately everything had gotten out of hand. Ineptly translating the words of the medieval student from Kraków, Maud had written to her, "The words of this letter will not fade, as long as you are in my heart." But didn't all words change in time inexorably to hatred, or worse, to a sort of dispassion? Gosia thought. She picked up the telephone again and dialed Vassily in New York. His machine came on, "Vassily Rostov, I cannot come to the telephone, please leave a message."

"Vassily, I'm calling from Houston."

"Gosia," Vassily broke through. "What a coincidence, I'm just reading Miłosz, and watching this little witch on the television. Here, let me turn off the answering machine. This little actress is in the shower, naked, showing her teeth to her boyfriend. He's just broken the shower-stall glass to get to her. She's hissing at him like a cat."

"I haven't time to watch television, dear, I'm having some people over for dinner to celebrate Lupe's show. I want to know if you sent those Man Ray photographs yet?"

"No, they're still in my suitcase. And have you read the Voinovich book I sent you?"

"I never read Russians, you know that. Vassily, I have to receive those photographs by next week. You're spreading yourself too thin. Half the time I can't reach you, and the other half of the time all you want to talk about is those Radar Sisters."

Vassily laughed. "Don't forget how I brought those Man Rays through customs without a hitch."

"That's true, dear. Are you going to be able to fly down for Lupe's show?"

"Too much business, but I know it will be beautiful. Send her my love, give her many kisses from me. It's strange, isn't it, how she's made Staś almost happy? No offense, sweetheart, I know you and Staś had another kind of pleasure, but Staś seems to be so talkative and full of ideas, almost hopeful. He told me he plays basketball, he seems almost robust."

"She is good for him. I wish he could be better for her, appreciate her more. I think he doesn't give in to his love for her. You see how he remains the same cool Staś, a little detached. He loves to immerse himself in her milieu, but somehow he remains bemused and distant."

"He's still in love with you."

"That's sweet of you to say. He is, and he isn't. But let's talk about Lupe. She's such a fascinating artist and person, quite stunning in every way. Most of my artists I wouldn't want to introduce to collectors, but her presence is really an asset. I'm even thinking of opening a branch in San Antonio if she'd like to keep an eye on it. It's just an idea."

"Staś doesn't seem to mind all the attention she's getting."

"I think he's relieved. He can just work in his studio and produce those yards and yards of uninterrupted meditation or speculation about existence or whatever it is, and not have to worry about showing. It was always such a pain for him to show; he always became so combative when the work wasn't 'understood' according to him."

"I think you're right. *¡Ay!,* now the girl is dressed again, and she's lying in bed with a cop, and her eye is bruised."

"Alright dear, I won't keep you, I have to start dinner."

"I wish I could be there. Yes, please give Lupe my love and kisses."

"Sweetheart," Gosia said.

"Sweetheart."

Gosia hung up and sat on her bed. She rubbed her forehead, then shook her head and went downstairs. Liszka followed. Gosia put on her coat, and went outside to the garden. It was only five o'clock, but already it was dark. Evening is always so dark in Texas, she thought, and now, unexpectedly, it had begun to snow. The flakes glistened in the wind. Gosia walked to the sage bush and bent down to break off a few sprigs. Each curled leaf carried a light load of snow. Gosia shook the branches, and returned to the kitchen. "Just like little ears," she said to herself, "these little sage leaves are like the small pointed ears of some lover. But who was it who had those ears?"

She busied herself with cooking; the roast lamb was almost done. She cut the sage leaves into a pan of melted butter. The leaves began to flatten and brown and to fill the room with a delicious fragrance. She made the salad and put the bread in to warm. Just then her son Wieńczysław came lightly down the stairs into the room. Gosia looked at him. He was a tall young man, as tall as she, but half as broad. In place of her strong, long nose, his was just a small upturned twist of flesh. Gosia's lips were broad and sensual; his formed a modest rosebud. Even her hands were longer and wider than his, her wrists thicker.

"Ah, here you are, dear," Gosia said. "Finished sleeping? Pour us some vodka. I'm putting out caviar. Where's Kazimierz, still sleeping?"

Wieńczysław nodded. He went to the refrigerator and poured the vodka into ice-cold glasses. Outside, guests were arriving. Headlights swung into the driveway. Gosia felt a pleasant sense of anticipation. She genuinely looked forward to this evening.

LUPE

VARIATIONS

Lupe dusted the light snow from the truck, and reached her hand into the air to let the snow touch her. She recognized Berto's car pulling into the driveway. Berto was an old Spanish poet whom Gosia always invited to her parties. Lupe wanted to be kind to Berto, so she waited for him in the driveway and they walked to the porch together. Under her arm she carried the parcel of fruit candy for Vassily.

"My dears," Gosia said, throwing open the door. "Dear Berto, let me take your hat before the snow melts on it." She lifted Berto's hat off his head and blew the snow off it. "Here dears, give me your coats. No, put them over there in the window seat. Lupe, what a beautiful blouse you're wearing." Gosia rested her hand lightly for a moment on the fabric over Lupe's breast.

Lupe had just purchased the pink rayon blouse that morning. She was so startled by Gosia's touch that she sighed involuntarily. "I brought the fruit," she said quickly.

"What fruit?"

"Oh, it's a present for Vassily, a sort of candy."

"Oh yes, too bad he couldn't be here. Here, let me put it away." Gosia took the parcel and put it into the refrigerator.

Now the other guests began to arrive: two collectors, a young medical student whom Gosia had met at a lecture, and the wealthy elderly couple who were lending Gosia their house in Houston for the winter.

Just as all the guests had taken off their coats, a handsome young man with a crewcut trotted downstairs. This was Kazimierz, an amateur boxer, a friend of Wieńczysław.

"A boxer?" Lupe asked with interest.

"Yes, you can call me Kaz," Kazimierz said.

By the time everyone sat down to dinner, Lupe felt that she was watching an elegant movie about rich people. Gosia carved the lamb, and kept the glasses filled. The conversation turned this way and that. "But I do miss Staś," Gosia said loudly. "In his honor, let's tell one of his interminable stories. What about the story about how Professor Pawliszewski gave Babka to Maciej and Staś? There were so many dogs in the Polish community at that time. I can tell the dog story as well as anyone. Or Lupe, you tell a story, the story about the trip to Mississippi."

Lupe suddenly had an urge to yawn. She politely stifled the yawn by turning her mouth into a little O. "Let's see," she said blushing. She could still feel the heat of Gosia's touch on her breast. She had been thinking about the time when one of her parochial school girlfriends and she had taken off their shirts and kissed each others' breasts just to see what it felt like. "It's good to practice being with boys," her girlfriend had said. Then she had slipped her hand inside

Lupe's underpants. "No, that's too realistic," Lupe had protested.

"Now let's see," Lupe said. "We were there in Long Beach, in a motel that had been destroyed by Hurricane Camille, and rebuilt. It was a bare place; Staś said there were twenty-one miles of bare sand. We talked about how we wanted to live there someday. Anyway, in the motel we got into an argument about something, I can't remember what, and we were going on and on when suddenly Staś looked at the ceiling and saw Poppin' Fresh. . . ."

"Who is Poppin' Fresh?" Berto interrupted.

"Haven't you seen Poppin' Fresh on TV?" Lupe asked. "He's that little man made of dough. A finger pokes him and he giggles. In any event, Staś saw something coming out of the ceiling, he saw the face of Poppin' Fresh. Actually it was the place where a light fixture used to be, painted white. He began to laugh, and he couldn't stop laughing. I got really mad at him. I wanted to murder him or divorce him."

Wieńczysław and Kazimierz laughed, but everyone else was quiet.

Lupe smiled at the young men sitting across from her.

"Berto, eat the *szpik*," Gosia said. "*Szpik*," Gosia explained to the other guests. "It's the marrow of the lambbone. It's delicious, but let's have a toast. To Lupe's show. *Na zdrowie!*" Everyone lifted their glasses of red wine.

"*Amor*," Berto cried.

Everyone laughed and drank deeply, and the conversation continued. Lupe could see that Gosia was flattering the potential purchasers of Lupe's paintings. The elderly couple were politely taking an interest in the young medical student. Lupe wanted to talk with Kazimierz and Wieńczysław, but Berto kept interrupting. He seemed to be trying to seduce her. "But how lovely you are, Lupe," he exclaimed. "Those breasts, and those high heels. You could walk all over me with those high heels." Lupe felt embarrassed in front of the two young men, and tried to change the subject.

After supper Gosia invited everyone into the living room, which was lit and warmed by a fire in a two-sided fireplace that opened onto both kitchen and living room. Everyone talked now about the dinner they had just eaten. Gosia's roast lamb with sage was pronounced to be even better than her chicken with fennel, and clearly so much less work. Gosia, handsome in dark slacks, seated herself in an armchair with high sides, and swung her long legs over one of the wings.

Kazimierz and Wieńczysław excused themselves and went off to their rooms to sleep so that they could be up early. They wanted to drive to Corpus the next day and walk on the beach. The elderly couple left. Gosia put on a cassette of Mexican dance music, tamped marijuana into her small ivory pipe, and passed it around the room. Everyone took deep drags. Gosia began to dance with the medical student, who whooped in imitation of the break in the male Mexican's singer's voice when he sang, "¡Ay ay!" In the room of dancers, Lupe with Berto, the art collectors drunkenly in each others' arms, Gosia was supreme. *Una reina*—she's like a queen in her house, Lupe thought, as she watched Gosia dance slowly, thigh to thigh with the medical student. The two glided in perfect synchronization back and forth across the floor.

From time to time Gosia called for more music, and

Lupe obliged by reversing the cassette. "Aren't you wonderful, Lupe," Gosia called. "More, more . . . more music!"

At midnight the collectors left. The medical student excused himself to go to the guest bathroom in a remote part of the house. Gosia maneuvered Lupe and Berto into the kitchen and whispered, "Please stay till he leaves."

"Who?" Berto asked.

"The medical student. I don't even know his name."

"But you seem so fond of him," Berto said.

"No, I don't even remember his name."

Suddenly neither Lupe nor Berto could remember his name either. When the nameless medical student returned, he announced that he had to get back to his studies. After he left, Berto, Gosia and Lupe sat down, weary, in three corners of the room, and were silent for some time. Then Gosia stood up and sat down on the couch with Berto. "Lupe, come over here," she said. "Let's all be friends. Sit with Berto and me." Now the two women sat with Berto between them.

"Why don't you sleep with Lupe," Berto said to Gosia. "She's so beautiful, so womanly."

"No," Gosia said, "Lupe should sleep with you, Berto. You've been after her all evening."

"Why don't we all sleep together?" Berto asked.

This is really like white people, Lupe thought. It's late at night, everyone is drunk. She didn't know what to say. Then Gosia leaned across Berto's chest—way across Berto's chest—and kissed Lupe on the lips. Lupe felt Gosia's hand touch her breast, drawing a slow circle. It seemed that Berto was patting her on the thigh. Berto took both women by the hand and escorted them downstairs into a bedroom. The three of them sat down together on the bed. Berto bent his large head over Gosia's thighs. He looks like an old burro, Lupe thought. This is all happening too quickly. The same thought seemed to cross Gosia's mind, because she suddenly laughed and said, "Why don't we just lie here." They sunk back into the pillows. Gosia took Lupe's hand and pressed it to her cheek. The Polish woman's skin was astonishingly smooth and warm. Lupe lay absolutely still; her heart was making a loud sound. Berto sighed and then began to snore softly and regularly. "Quiet," Gosia whispered, "don't wake him. We'll go to the kitchen and get some coffee."

DISAPPOINTMENTS

Plates and glasses were piled all over Gosia's kitchen.

"Berto looked like an old warhorse called back into battle. Poor dear," Gosia said.

"I was thinking the same thing myself," Lupe said.

Gosia bent and looked into the refrigerator. She is so very tall, Lupe thought.

"I could eat a lamb sandwich," Gosia said. "And what is this that you've brought for Vassily?"

"You can open it," Lupe said.

Gosia unwrapped the package on the counter. "Oh it's fruit, how sexual, the bananas, these round things."

"No no, it's just fruit. Candies."

"The coffee will be ready in a minute," Gosia said. She sat down at the table. "You like Vassily really quite a bit, don't you?"

"Oh no," Lupe said. "Just as a friend."

"Vassily, he could have done so much, he's from the

Russian intelligensia, you know. He could have distinguished himself, but he's always onto some new harebrained scheme. He wanders about the world. He's a boy, he's a child."

"And Staś," Gosia continued, "I could have loved him, but underneath his romanticism, he's cold. You're much better for him than I was. He can't see beyond himself. But you don't have that problem with him, do you?"

"No, not really," Lupe said.

"Staś believes in the melancholy of middle age; he thinks melancholy is an appropriate response to the tragedy of life. But for me life is not always tragic, it is also beautiful, and it offers so many pleasures to enjoy. Staś is too depressed. I know he thinks that I avoid pain, that I'm not acting my age. As he and I grow older, we seem to grow further apart, to agree less and less about anything."

Lupe searched in her mind for a new topic. "*Wracasz do Polski*? Will you go back to Poland?" she asked politely.

"Ah, I see Staś has been teaching you a little Polish."

"That's the only phrase I know."

"No, I won't go back to Poland. It's a sad place. We all carry Poland within us. I'm sure you do too."

"Hmm, yes," Lupe said.

"After we have our coffee, would you like to come upstairs to see the prints in my room?"

"Oh yes, I would like that, that would please me very much," Lupe said.

GOSIA'S ROOM

"To make love is to create a lace, a veil which reveals everything and nothing," Gosia said. She was sitting on her bed.

Lupe was examining a Japanese print on Gosia's wall. Was it an original? A reproduction? A man with a very wrinkly penis was making love to a young woman who held a fan over her face. The man's penis looked like an old man's face, or a very old rock, or perhaps a mushroom with many furrows in it. "But do Japanese men really look like this? Are they so different, or is it just the style of drawing?" Lupe asked.

"A mixture of both," Gosia said. "You know, I'm sure you would look lovely in my ruby earrings. Try these on."

Lupe went over to the bed and leaned down. Gosia lifted Lupe's earrings from her ears, and hung her own rubies in Lupe's earlobes. "Come here, Liszka," Gosia said, patting the bed. "Jump up. Doesn't Lupe look lovely in these earrings? Look in the mirror, dear."

Lupe sat down at the dressing table. "They look beautiful," Lupe said. "But you mean you let your dog get on your bed?"

"She always sleeps with me, at the bottom of the bed of course."

"Your room is full of so many fine things," Lupe said. She looked at Gosia's lipstick on the table. "Your lipstick is so dark, so much redder than mine."

"Try it on," Gosia said.

Lupe picked up the open lipstick from the dressing table. She felt weak. "Ah no," she said, "I'd better not. There are so many interesting things in this room. Staś just has Polish things in our room, photographs of his father and grandfather in military uniforms, with moustaches."

"Staś is a little too Polish at times, don't you think?" Gosia said. "Come sit on the bed and tell me your real name."

Lupe sat down on the edge of the bed. "Maria. Maria Guadalupe," she said.

"I was so moved by your name when I called to get the announcements printed. Maria Guadalupe. Lovely. Tell me dear, have you ever been in bed with a woman?"

"Well yes, once, I mean I always slept with my sisters."

"But I mean a woman who wants to make love with you."

"Yes, that once, I was just thinking of it tonight. I was with a school friend."

"It's especially tender, isn't it, to be with a woman?"

"I remember, it was so very hot that day, the window was open, the wind came in lightly to touch our skins."

"And did it feel wonderful?"

"Oh yes, it did, but I was a little embarrassed, or shy. I didn't want to go too far."

"Just lightly, you wanted just lightly to be touched?"

"Yes, and have the curtains rise up. The wind was so cool, and the curtains would blow—"

"Lupe, why don't you lie down, and I'll rub your back. You must be tired from walking in those shoes."

Lupe lay down. She felt pleasantly sleepy and at ease. She felt Gosia touch the nape of her neck and unbutton her blouse and skirt.

"Here, I want to stroke these muscles," Gosia said. "These are the sexual muscles, the gluteus maximus. If I rub these, you will feel completely relaxed. Or perhaps I'll just gently graze my teeth over those muscles."

Lupe felt Gosia bend over her; she felt Gosia's brilliant white teeth pass lightly over her skin. Gosia's teeth seemed to touch Lupe's very nerves. Lupe laughed, rather more shrilly than she intended. "Don't, I feel like you're going to eat me, I'm ticklish," she said, laughing almost uncontrollably.

"Oh no, darling, I won't do that. I won't eat you, darling, lie still."

"No, I can't take it," Lupe said. She turned over. "Kiss me again, as we did downstairs, kiss me."

THE OPENING

The opening night of the exhibition Lupe wore her red dress, with the ruby earrings that Gosia had lent her for the occasion.

"Sensational," Gosia said. "But where have I seen that dress?" They were standing alone in the gallery, an hour before the show was to open.

"The photo," Lupe answered. "Remember the photo Vassily took of this dress?"

"Ah yes, dear," Gosia said.

Lupe went into the office to do something. But what was it, she couldn't remember. She heard Gosia walk in behind her. She was about to turn when she felt the touch of silk as Gosia embraced her from behind. She felt Gosia's hand come to rest on her thigh. At that moment the bell rang. A boy was at the door. The two women separated. The boy had flowers from Staś and from Vassily. The guests began to arrive.

"Give yourself to it," Gosia said. "Let's have a drink, it's your night."

THE CHILDREN

Lupe was sitting at the big desk at La Arena for the day. The gallery was quiet. Lupe was thinking, Gosia's touch seemed to have burned into her flesh. Gosia had such large hands that when she held Lupe, her hands extended from Lupe's elbow to Lupe's shoulder. Lupe had instantly grasped that this was not a permanent love: This was a moment, like the day when she and Staś had followed the Little Plata down to the Guadalupe. Where the two rivers joined, there was a dazzling limestone bluff. They had taken off their clothes and slipped into the water, which was so soft, light green and swift. They lay in the strong current, holding onto cypress roots, so as not to be swept away. "This water is celadon," Lupe had whispered to Staś.

One couldn't live like that all the time, but such moments were to be held in one's heart. Lupe remembered this morning waking up with Gosia.

125

"In two weeks I'll be going home," she had said as they lay in bed. "I'll be sad to leave you."

"I'll be sad too," Gosia said.

"What if I stayed here with you?" Lupe ventured.

"Oh no, dear," Gosia smiled. "Really, your life is with Staś. Our time now is a dear interlude but our lives will have to go on eventually. There are people I have to flirt with in my line of business. It's exhausting and not satisfying, but that's how it is. You and I will always love each other and be in touch. Don't ever tell Staś about this. We'll never tell Staś, and in this way we can all always be friends."

Yes, this is right, Lupe thought to herself. She watched Gosia get up and walk to her closet. "Staś always tries to make order out of things," Lupe said.

"Yes," Gosia said. "He's always trying to tie everything together, every part of his past to his present. To my mind he's trying to make an impossible synthesis. He should just let go a little more. Here, dear, help me select which blouse to wear. Do you think this one?" Gosia held up a silk blouse.

"That would be nice."

Gosia took five blouses out and laid them on the bed: violet, green, silver lamé, pale blue, and a cooler cobalt blue.

"I choose the green," Lupe said.

"Do you think I'll look like a cadaver?"

"A what?"

"A corpse, a dead person, in green?"

"Oh no," Lupe remembered, reassuring Gosia, "you will look beautiful."

Now as Lupe sat in Gosia's chair at the gallery, she thought again about the word *synthesis,* with its magical almost hissing sound. From moment to moment everything seemed confusing at times, but when you looked backwards on life, it usually made some sort of sense. She felt content, content with Gosia, content with Staś, content to be sitting here with the silence and passion of her paintings surrounding her, the grays, the gray-greens, the matte surfaces, the built-up areas where she had mixed sand into the paint. A group of school children had come into the gallery earlier. On impulse she decided to try to reach Staś at home and tell him about it.

"Yes, they gathered all around that gray vertical painting. They loved it, they were so quiet, all big eyes. One little black kid stepped up to me. He said, 'I can draw real well. I'm going to be an artist.' "

"*¡Qué bueno!*," Staś said happily.

"Yes, how good," Lupe said.

STAŚ

SPRING SNOW

The day after Lupe's call, Maciej brought Babka out to Staś. A dusting of snow covered the ground. Staś and Maciej stood outside in the yard. Maciej stroked Babka with one hand, while with the other he threw millet onto the snow. Some sparrows shot down from the ash-leaf maple and began quarreling, raising small clouds of the light powder.

"Soon your wife will be here. Heart and head will be one for you," Staś said. "Take care, you're Lupe's and my *basso continuo*."

"Ah yes, how do you say, running bass," Maciej said.

"You're becoming so American," Staś laughed. He watched Maciej drive away across the bridge in a big American car he had borrowed. The sparrows flew up into the trees again, and a few perched along the sunny ridgepole of the barn.

It seemed to Staś that Babka was happy to be at the ranch. She followed him down to the river, and watched him shake the snow from the hammock. Then, seeing that Staś was going to stay in the hammock for a while, she walked carefully down over the stones to the river's edge and drank water. Then she returned and lay down a few feet from Staś.

"Poor human beings," Staś said, "caught in a web of passion. Now Babka, I want to tell you of the odd things that have been happening around here. I went for a walk and ran into a raccoon almost as big as you on the ranch road. It was walking the other way in the daylight and showed no fear of me till the last minute, when it scurried into a culvert. And it has been reported in town that bands of raccoons are wandering around. Five or six raccoons walked into a woman's garage in the noontime. Perhaps it is a sign of Apocalypse. And then we have the fact that one-third of all babies born today must be delivered by Caesarean. They are simply too big."

Babka listened attentively, and seemed to accept everything that Staś said. "Here Granny, it's cold, let's go to the house." Babka slowly rose and followed Staś to the house, and made herself comfortable on the kitchen floor. Staś noticed the white gladioli. He looked at them arranged in an arc against the framed white landscape in the window. The spent blooms on the lower part of the stalks looked like folded kidskin gloves. Staś hesitated to pick them. It was something Lupe usually did, remove the dying blooms. He appreciated the touch of color they lent to the otherwise monochrome composition. Staś decided to let the flowers be, and gazed out the window at the sparrows on the snow while Babka slept.

TWO TELEPHONE CALLS

Staś pulled the covers up around him. It was one of those cold nights in early February. The telephone rang.

"Hello?" Staś said. "Wait, I have papers all over the bed."

"It's Vassily. How are you, *querido?* I'm in Atlantic City, and I have a deal for you. It's gold. We can make a quick fortune in gold. Right now. I just met this Dr. Buey—"

Staś said, "Buey?"

Vassily said, "Yes, here, take a pencil and write it down." As Vassily spelled out the name, his voice faded away until it could not be heard. The phone went dead. Staś hung up, and waited, but Vassily did not call back. Staś put down his pen. The phone rang again. It was Lupe.

"Staszek, are you alright? Are you gloomy?"

"I'm fine, *amor*. And you?"

"I've sold two paintings. What have you been doing? How is the stock market?"

"I like to employ the technique of small repeated gains. Compaq options 15 to 17, and 16 to 18. And we've made a killing in pharmaceuticals and biotech, particularly that ICN. I bought it at 20 and it went to 30 in a week. I sold at 30, now it's back at 22."

"That's good Staś, but I want you to stop buying now. Back off. Get off the margin. Your vein has been lit up for too long, the vein of gambling and addiction. It's swollen. You know what vein it is, it's the big one in your *pene*."

"Ah, maybe you're right."

"You know, it's like the pie that lights up on the game show."

"What pie?" Staś asked.

"You know, when one section of the circle lights up, then the contestant asks the question."

"Oh yes. And are you safe in Houston? Are you getting enough sleep."

"I'm fine. And how is Babka?"

"She's very well."

"And I know you and Maciej are talking about Babka and all those Polish dogs all the time."

"No, really we're not. Maciej went to Dallas. Babka is here with me. I'm talking with Babka."

"Good. Are you painting? I'm meeting a rich *gringo* tomorrow who might buy an etching."

"*Fantastico,*" Staś said. "Yes, I've been painting. In the studio it's as if I walk in and schools of fish swim by me, around me. But you know, sometimes I don't want to go in there; I hate to start painting, but once I'm in there it's like being in a river. Then I had a funny call the other day. A guy who wants success badly called to explain his new theory of how to sell paintings. Have cocktail parties, he said, get a fashionable coat, wear it, send a taxi for an influential critic. And all I could think of was to cook a beet. I thought why not roast a beet in foil, roast it in the oven and serve a roasted beet."

"Have you been eating well?"

"Yes, have you? I'm going to send you a check tomorrow."

"*¡Ay! amor,*" Lupe sighed, "I don't need any money now. Staś, there's something I want to tell you."

"Yes?"

"Staś, I feel closer to you—I love you—more than anyone on earth," Lupe said.

"Lupe, *querida,*" Staś said.

A KILLING
IN GOLD

Staś found one of Lupe's combs by the river. He picked it up and put it in his pocket. He pictured her sitting, perhaps with her feet in the water, rising up, forgetting the comb. When he returned to the house, Staś went inside. He looked out the window and saw that Babka still stood on the lawn, four square, expectant, waiting for Staś to come out again. But when he didn't reappear, she went back to the river to drink, and then lay down under the pecan trees.

Inside the house Staś heard an irritating noise that was hard to identify. It was the new remote phone that he had just installed. Staś picked it up. He walked outside with the phone.

"Hello?"

"Vassily."

"Rostov?"

"*Sí.*"

Staś walked around to the back of the house and sat down in the deck chair.

"I have a new remote phone," he said, "touchtone and pulse, to get programmed stock quotes. I'm sitting outdoors."

"*¡Que bueno!*" Vassily said. "I must apologize for hanging up on you. While we were talking, a beautiful woman—she has a Ph.D., she's a CEO at an important company, I can't say which—she was lifting her skirt and kissing me in the phone booth."

"Say no more," Staś said, "I know you're making a killing in gold."

"*Sí amigo.* How's Lupe? How can you two spend so much time apart?"

"A habit. When she was little, her *padre* went to Chicago eight months a year to work, then he brought home the money to the family in Nogales. The same with me. My father was always in London working for the Polish government-in-exile; he'd be at home with us in Washington a few months a year. You remember?"

"Yes. But how is Lupe?"

"She's so happy with her show. She asks after you. And Maciej also. I have a letter from him from Dallas. Here, I'll read it to you. 'Dear Staś, I realize as I wait for my wife that once in a lifetime we meet the person who is right for us. I called home. Mother and Father are fine. It's unusually cold in Warsaw. Sister goes to Hungary next week. I am at the airport waiting for plane.' Then he goes on to say that he and his wife might go back to Warsaw to try to sell their apartment. Then they plan to return and apply for U.S. citizenship."

"Risky to go back," Vassily said.

"I know."

"Pero, adiós, amigo, espero verte pronto."

"Adiós, y suerte," Staś said.

THE NIGHT BLOOMING

Late in the afternoon Staś was still sitting in the backyard by Lupe's herb garden, working on a translation of a poem from French into Polish for a friend with whom he had a correspondence. Papers, dictionaries and xerox copies were arranged about him.

"The important word is *'modulant,'* meaning to pass from one key to another," Staś said. His eyes rested on Babka. She lay a few feet distant, in the stripe of shadow cast by the chimney of the house.

"Remember, Babka?" he said warmly. "Do you recall when you used to be away for a few days? You would just take off. Or sometimes you'd bring your gentleman friends here. We'd wake in the morning and find a collie here with you. With what slow undulating movements you made love with those guys, and all the time you seemed to look far off into the empyrean. Even when afterwards you both stood, ridiculously bound together, I saw the infinite in your eyes. Remember, Lupe ran out once and cried, 'Staś, the copulatory tie, could it happen to us?' 'I don't think so,' I said. And just then you and your collie came undone, and you two took off to chase up and down the pasture. And now you are old, you spend most of your day under the porch where the dirt is fresh and cool."

Babka didn't move, but listened intently to Staś. Just then a live oak leaf twirled down through the air to land on Babka's back. Babka looked around at the leaf on her back, and rolled over on her side. She extended her front paw out towards Staś playfully.

Staś felt the need to make a conscious analogy.

"Watching you pass through the ages of your life is like hearing one musical phrase in many different keys," he said to Babka. "Or perhaps it is like experiencing the same language in differing dialects."

Staś was remembering the trip that he and Vassily had taken to Miami some years ago, and the Cuban woman with whom he had had an affair. Gradually Staś's Spanish had taken on the inflections of Cuba, then Colombia— because of all those Colombians that were in and out of their hotel rooms. The blonde Cuban woman and Staś fought endlessly about where to go, what to wear, whom to see. Staś remembered this period of his life with a feeling of exhaustion. Then Lupe had entered his life, and a sweet domesticity settled over him. He was puzzled and fascinated by his wife. He loved her Nogales delivery of the Spanish tongue. He could speak Castilian, Cuban and Colombian Spanish, but now he preferred to speak with the inflections of Lupe's Monterrey cousins, and Lupe's sisters. He even enjoyed speaking a mixture of Spanish and English in the San Antonio manner.

And Lupe, in turn, was amused by American expressions. Recently he had asked Lupe, "What are you eating?"

"Cup o' bean," Lupe had answered.

"What's that?" Staś asked.

"Isn't that how white people talk?" Lupe asked innocently. "If you have a cup of something, you say 'cup o'.' I see it written everywhere."

It must be that human beings enchanted each other, Staś decided. Perhaps that's what marriage was—an enchantment. And perhaps he amused Lupe in some way also.

Staś lay back in his deck chair in silence for several minutes. Then he arched his head back and looked up at the sky through the leaves.

"Ecstasy," Staś said. Babka sat up and listened. "You hear the loll loll loll, the chinkling, burbling sound of the river going along, but then every once in a while the river rises to a roar. Perhaps like last night, Babka. I had put you in the barn when I went to town to see a movie. You looked at me in silence, as if embarrassed for me that I would treat you like a dog. But what could I do, I didn't want you wandering up to the road. You're too old to be out in the dark. Then when I returned from town, all was forgiven, you leaped about and insisted that I scratch your ears. Then we went to the house, the dark steps. We found the right key, entered the house, and it was paradise, the fragrance filled the entire house. The night-blooming cereus was blooming, that enormous white flower with the pathway of pollen down into its depths. I try to imagine the incredible tropical bird or insect that pollinates such a flower. We went into the living room with the flashlight, and looked at the flower. That's how it is, four or five times a year.

"The next morning everything's back to normal, the flower dangling straight down like a twisted rope. Already I'm thinking ahead, to the next time, the next time."

THE BLOW

Staś found that he couldn't sleep. He lay in bed and thought about the night-blooming cereus. He decided to call Lupe at her sister's house in Houston, even though it was almost 1 A.M.

"My apologies," he said. "Is Lupe there?"

"She's not here Staś, she's been staying over with the gallery woman."

"Ah, Gosia."

"Yes, that tall woman who runs the gallery."

"Oh, sorry to disturb you."

"That's alright Staś, are you coming over to visit?"

"Well no, I've been a little sick. Listen, don't tell Lupe I called. It's nothing important."

"Alright Staś. Good night."

Staś put down the phone and sat still. He felt a horrible sense of alarm in his chest. He decided to call Maciej in Dallas.

"*Halo*," Maciej said sleepily.

"It's Staś. Are you angry that I called so late?"

"Of course not, friend, what is it?"

"Lupe's having an affair with Gosia."

"Oh," Maciej said, pausing. Staś waited. "Staś, don't let Lupe know that you know this," Maciej said.

"Of course not, I'm a gentleman. We have an agreement; we made our agreement some time ago. But how can Gosia do this? She's so frivolous, she's bored, she has nothing to do in her life, she doesn't even work for *Solidarność* anymore. When the American Congress makes a mistake and I have to write to them, she never signs the letter with me."

"Staś," Maciej said.

"And furthermore, Lupe's just a child, she's an innocent young girl, she's never been with anyone but me. And what could they do anyway? I don't believe it. What could there be to it?"

"Maybe it makes Gosia feel young again for a minute. Maybe it is an exchange of innocence and experience. Perhaps they only hug each other. It's nothing to worry about, Staś. It's part of Lupe going out into world, she needs to take steps by herself."

"Ah, perhaps you're right," Staś said, "innocence and experience. But I feel hurt and left out. I shouldn't have run around so much myself. I feel remorse."

"Remorse? What is that?"

"*Remordere*. To bite again, regret, *żal*. I feel terrible. Could it be I feel remorse?"

"It sounds like something that a happy person feels. Aren't you too depressed to feel remorse?"

"No, I think I feel very bad, I feel remorseful."

"Perhaps it was not always right that you ran around?

We can joke about wearing many hats, but look at me. Since I am married, I am faithful. My wife and I plan children. This will be good for you Staś; children will teach you new ways to live."

"Perhaps, but what is it I feel?"

"Don't dwell on it, don't even think about it. It's something Lupe does for herself, something you don't know about. Don't trouble your heart. Let Babka heal you. She will."

Staś sighed.

"Call me if you can't sleep."

"I will. Thanks friend."

Staś hung up. His heart hurt. He did not dare to look around the room. He knew that so many things in the room—especially the objects scattered over Lupe's night table—would remind him of Lupe. Outside the circle of light cast by his bedlamp, there were photographs on the walls of his father and grandfather, portraits of Lupe's grandparents and uncles, a photo of Concepción as a young girl, walking in Monterrey. Staś could not bear to look into the semidarkness. Instead he stared down at the striped cotton bedspread that Lupe had brought from Mexico. He ran his fingers over the coarse cotton. How could Lupe be in any arms other than his?

THE BEAUTY
OF
IMPLEMENTS

Staś closed the book he had been reading and pushed it away from him. It was a recurring nightmare, or rather daymare, that suddenly everything dear would be taken from him. He put his head down on the kitchen table. He covered his head with his arms. Babka, too, covered her head as best she could with one paw. She slept in the bright counterpane of sunlight that spread over the kitchen floor. Sunlight played through the prism hanging on a thread high in the window. Ovals of pure chromatic colors flitted across the cabinets and walls on the darker side of the room as the prism slowly turned this way and that.

The image of the church at Panna Maria entered Staś's mind. He remembered the first time he and Lupe and Concepción had visited there. Concepción had stopped to light a candle at the back of the church while Staś and Lupe had walked down the center aisle, pausing every few steps to admire the stained-glass windows given to the church by the different Polish families of the town. There was something simple and honest about the little church. Staś remembered kneeling at the communion rail with Lupe and saying prayers in the vulgate Latin of his childhood.

Now Staś imagined himself back again in Panna Maria with Lupe, at that time when they were newly married. Staś felt his eyes fill with tears. The tears wet his face. His heart grew lighter as he pictured the colors from the stained-glass windows falling on Lupe and himself. Staś cried quietly for some time. Then he roused himself. Simultaneously man and dog stood up.

"I'll cut down the corn today," Staś said. Babka followed Staś outdoors. The sunlight was dazzling. Staś's neighbors always invited Staś to grow corn in the middle of their field. No trouble at all, they said, to leave a strip down the center for him. Staś had thanked them, but said no, that he wanted to put in his own corn and hoe it up himself. A large portion of Staś's garden was given over to corn, and it was time to cut down the papery brown leaves and stalks to be plowed under.

"A scythe is really a man," Staś explained to Babka as they walked to the barn. "Or perhaps a man is a scythe, for when he picks up a scythe, he begins to resemble the scythe. When he works with it, he becomes the sweep and curve of the scythe." Staś selected a scythe from his collection. He had a handsome one he very much esteemed. Curved wooden tines extended from the handle, parallel to the blade, so that one could cradle aside the load at each sweep. But today Staś selected the angular knobby-handled scythe that looked like a raw-boned country boy. He and Babka went out to the garden. Babka lay down in the shade of the house and watched Staś from a distance.

"Remember how those raccoons used to chatter and chuckle in the bushes while I was hilling up the corn?" Staś said. "And look, now they've had their fill." The few small nubbin ears that Staś had left in the field had been nibbled to the cobs by the raccoons. Staś laid the cut stalks in neat rows. As he worked, he thought about the beauty of implements, and his imagination seized upon the hoe, the instrument of hope, the tool most associated with the spring of the year, planting, cultivation.

"Turn a hoe just so, and you may scratch a line in the earth for the seed, and a little more of an angle, and you cover the seed," Staś said. "Then you chop with your hoe all summer, you pull up earth around each plant. You break the soil, transport it on your hoe hooked just so. Possibly the hoe is the most versatile and yet simple implement on earth. I have seen some giant hoes in the South, like the cotton hoe."

Babka listened.

"Perhaps," Staś continued, "tools are our best comfort. The most beautiful are those that closely resemble pointed sticks, or a rock attached to a stick. I remember once riding on the subway in New York. Some guys got on with massive implements almost as tall as themselves with which to fix the tracks, huge bars of steel with only the slightest articulation. They were artifacts from prehistory."

Staś paused. "Hmmmhmm, it's hot working. Now look at all this corn lying down." Babka and Staś surveyed the flattened stalks.

"All very good," Staś said. Babka followed Staś around the house to the barn. It was late afternoon. The earth and air were swiftly cooling. Staś wiped the scythe with a cloth and put it away.

"Want to play? Come on," Staś said. Babka bowed down, putting the front part of her body close to the ground and challenged Staś to begin. For several minutes dog and man circled each other, with intervals of silent deliberation. Staś's task was to capture Babka and force her to lie down. Eventually Staś did just that. Babka lay panting in mock surrender under the weight of Staś's arms.

"Beloved monster," Staś said, and then they both sprang up, and began all over again.

SAEPE

Staś looked through the house for Virgil's *Georgics*. He found the book, opened it, and was shocked to find a passage that he had never noticed before, even though he often read to Babka about beekeeping and husbandry and tilling. He sat at the kitchen table and translated the passage for Babka: "Nor let the care of dogs be farthest in your thoughts, but give the speedy Spartan pups and fierce Molossians rich whey. Never, with them guarding your stables, need you fear a night robber, or an attack by wolves, or restless Spaniards behind your back. Often you will chase the timid ass, and hunt the rabbit with dogs, and the doe. Often you will rouse with barking the wild boar from the woods, and with loud baying on high mountains drive the buck-deer into the nets . . . ," Staś paused. *"Saepe, saepe,"* he said to Babka, "these are the key words, my dear friend."

Staś took out a piece of paper and put it on the table. "The more time I spend alone, the more I feel I am disintegrating," he said to Babka. He made some further notes:

> **bought today ICN—2000 @ 18⅜.**
> **1000 @ 18¼**
> **in one week expect 5 or 6 points**
> **check oil   check transm fluid**
> **return books to library**

Staś adjusted his chair.

"And what are the possibilities, the odds?" he asked. He wrote down a few:

> **Lupe and I have a child, which surprises us both. In addition we adopt some Mexican children and move to Mexico.**

> **Maciej and his family settle in the US and become citizens.**

> **I die in an accident.**

> **Vassily dies. His liver gives out.**

> **Lupe stays in Houston with Gosia.**

> **Lupe leaves me for another white guy more willing to father children. I live the rest of my life in a state of gloom.**

> **Gosia lives on.**

Staś stood up and went to the kitchen phone and called Lupe. She was at the gallery. "I want you to come home," he said.

"I want to, Staś. I see now how much you love me, how detailed your love is for me. No one loves me as you do. I'll put on a special dark eyeliner for you. I'll leave tomorrow morning, early."

LENTE

It was 6 A.M., and a mourning dove was just beginning to coo under the eaves above the windows of the bedroom, two walls of which Lupe had painted white, leaving the two original stenciled walls unpainted. A generation ago, a craftsman had stenciled the house with birds and flowers. Now the red swags in the black borders had faded, but the flowers and birds stood out boldly. Their room was really not very different from the painted rooms where they had stayed in Mexico.

The phone rang.

"*Amor,*" Lupe said. "Are your hairs curled up real tight?"

"Lupe, where are you?"

"Half way home."

"But I can't wait to see you, to hear your sharp tongue. First you'll be sniffing around the house to see if any other woman has been here. Then, once you're satisfied you'll warm up."

"Yes, Staś, I will. I'll see you so soon. I'm going to get a cup of coffee. Don't run any machines today. Just wait for me to come. Don't buy any stocks."

"*Bueno mi flor, flor de mi vida.*"

"*Adiós.*" Lupe hung up.

After many miles of traveling, Lupe will be tired, Staś thought. Should he make breakfast? He tried to picture it all, the car clattering over the bridge, perhaps about 9 A.M. The cats will run out to greet her, he thought. His mind leapt ahead to the moment when he and Lupe would get into bed, and then—*lente, lente*—they would enter, each through the other, their native country. Already, in his imagination, he felt himself slowly entering her, fractions of an inch at a time, slowly entering as if to make up for the lost days, slowly climbing the spiral stair, returning to himself, to her, to earth from the giddy state of suspension he had been in since they parted. Already, tenderly, he was entering her, slowly so that time was slowing also and would never end. He felt himself settle on the earth, one foot, then the other. He felt the ground, he felt his weight again on his legs, he began to walk, he began to run through the high grass of a green field.

HOME

Staś emerged from the canopy of green leaves. He had been swinging in the hammock in the ash-leaf maple grove by the river. He stamped his foot and startled Lupe.

"¡Ay!, Staś," she said. "You've been sleeping again in your solitary hammock. Why don't you put up the big colorful hammock between the trees instead of sneaking off and sleeping like a soldier in that skinny little hammock? And what are you doing sleeping in the middle of the day? Here I am working, transplanting the cilantro plants."

"I'm like that herd of cattle in Shakespeare that stays under the trees at midday. And anyway, isn't every Mexican woman secretly proud of her lazy husband?"

"I'm not listening to this nonsense," Lupe said and continued ferociously pulling weeds.

'Lupe," Staś said, "it's so wonderful to have you here. Last night when I was walking in the yard, I saw you pass by the window upstairs. I'm so happy you're here, let's get remarried. We could have a private ceremony for ourselves."

"And then a big party. A good idea," Lupe said. "I want to wait till as many of our friends as possible can come."

"The private ceremony we'll have in the river," Staś said. "We'll stand in the river and make love."

"We'll see," said Lupe. "What are you doing now? I thought you were going to call your broker today."

"That's right. The Avon put, July 30. I bought 10 puts at ½, they sunk to ⅜, to ¼. I put a stop on them at 1. I don't feel hopeful about it though."

"Well, go call him." Staś went indoors and called his broker.

"Three-fifths to one-half," his broker said.

"Okay," Staś said, "thanks." Then he dialed his analyst.

"Hello," said the analyst.

"Doctor," said Staś.

"How's everything, Staś?"

"Fine, but I keep falling asleep."

"These seizures," Dr. Ransom said, "are like small epileptic attacks. After any especially pleasureable—or frightening and unpleasureable—event, you can expect to fall asleep. Enjoy it, it's a form of release."

"After all, being awake isn't always the happiest state of affairs," Staś said. "I often feel like Dante, swooning at the end of each canto. Now I'm in Paradise. I want to wreathe a summer around my wife and myself such as we have never had, perhaps will never have again."

"I understand," Dr. Ransom said. "I'm happy for you Staś."

Staś and the doctor talked for another twenty minutes. Then Staś went outdoors to the barn and got the long-handled spade he liked, and carried it to the back of the house where he started digging to enlarge his garden.

TO GRIEVE
AGAIN

Staś drove down to Houston for his next session with his analyst; also to see Vassily, who was going to be in town.

"And is it quite right with Lupe again?" Dr. Ransom asked.

"Oh yes, better than before, somehow," Staś said.

"And what do you think these days about Gosia?"

"Those kisses so redolent of Poland, opium, vodka, cigarettes, printed silk, autumn—"

"What does redolent mean?" Dr. Ransom asked.

"*Olor,* fragrant with, olorous, dolorous. I don't know. To grieve again, perhaps. There was a time when Gosia's handwriting alone could bring tears to my eyes," Staś said. "I don't want to think about it. I want to be a good husband to Lupe. I'm tired of running around."

"Go on."

"I feel hopeful."

"Perhaps it's not only because Lupe's back with you,

but because you've finally put Gosia to one side, laid to rest all the memories that she represents."

"Yes. Gosia, she was a tie to my past. She was my lifeline to the old Poland. Now I guess Maciej has replaced her, to an extent. He's a connection to a newer Poland. With Vassily I'm always on guard. It's as if we have to show off to each other. I always feel as if I'm sparring with Gosia and Vassily."

"Perhaps you feel closer to Maciej and Lupe right now."

"Yes, I do. But Gosia, Vassily, Lupe, Maciej and I will always contain each other. We are all parts of each other."

Later in the day Staś drove to Lupe's sister's house. They ate rice with squid. Then she made him a bed on the couch, and Staś stayed up late watching TV. The next morning he saw Stefanie Powers being interviewed on a Spanish-speaking station.

"But look, she speaks perfect Spanish," Lupe's sister said. "Yes, she speaks four or five languages," Staś said. Lupe's sister finished putting on her makeup and left as Staś was calling his broker.

"Better lower the stop on the Avon Products–July 30 call to ¾," Staś said. "That's AVPSF. And I want to buy 20 calls on IBM, October 165, if you can pick them up at 2 right away."

"Wait a minute," the broker said. "Let me check. It's at 143 right now. Yes, if it goes to 150 you can sell the calls at 4."

"Good," Staś said. "Try to get those 20 at 2."

Staś rode across the city in a taxi to meet Vassily for breakfast. Again he ate squid. This time it was a ceviche of rice and squid, with plantain.

"Women who don't like squid don't like sex," Vassily said.

"Well look, Gosia doesn't like squid," Staś said.

"Perhaps that says something," Vassily replied. "I mean, she never did want to live with you."

"Yes, we were like two animals that kicked each other away after sex."

"*¡Ay!, pero,* exactly," Vassily said. "And yet, she couldn't live without you. She used to tell me it was your chestnut-colored hair."

"Well look, I can't think about this anymore. Tell me about your Fury," Staś said.

"It looks like a '55 car, but it's a '67. This is a car to glide around in, in the night. The theme is gold. The interior has a gold stripe that runs all around it, and this stripe even runs under and around the dashboard. And there are gold medallions all over the interior."

Vassily went on at length to describe the car and to tell Staś about the land he was thinking of buying in Bahia, in Brazil.

"*Pero amigo,* I must go," Vassily said. "Here are the drawings for the Radon Sisters' costumes." He took a thick sheaf of xerox copies out of a black canvas bag on the chair beside him. "Let me know what you think."

They walked over to Lupe's sister's building, where Staś had left his car in the lot. "You'll come to take the photos of Lupe in the Fury soon?" Staś asked.

"*Sí, compadre,* you know me, I'm *peregrino,* a wanderer. I'll come as soon as possible. Goodbye for now."

HASTE TO THE WEDDING

Staś drove home from Houston. All the way home, white petals were falling from the trees, almost as if it were snowing. Staś slept that night like a child.

The next day Lupe and Staś drove to a wedding. Their neighbors half a mile down the river had a daughter who was getting married. They drove over the dusty ranch road to the church. Again the white blossoms were falling from the trees. Everywhere, the trees were in bloom as they drove to the small church in the sparsely populated town.

The bride and groom took communion. They promised to forsake all others. When the minister pronounced them man and wife, the groom bent the bride backwards with a passionate kiss. The congregation clapped hesitantly. The minister beamed, and then the people broke into unabashed clapping for the bride and groom, who still lingered in the kiss.

After the wedding, the guests drove to the bride's

parents' ranch which was a few miles away. Some children from a local agricultural club bustled around, preparing to serve the meal. Lupe looked exquisite in her dark blue dress and white shawl. Staś noticed that she was getting a silver patch in her black hair, a stripe of silver on the left side, like her mother. Staś was dressed in gray with a narrow black tie. They decided to sit under the large yellow tent outdoors and Lupe led Staś to the furthest table, which was right beside a grove of locust trees. White petals drifted down onto the grass. A fine breeze stirred the paper tablecloths. Presently all the tables filled up, and the children from the agricultural club brought big platters of home-cooked food to the tables. Lupe turned graciously to this side and that, answering questions directed to her about the instruction of Spanish in the local schools.

Staś went to get some punch. Music flowed from the windows.

"There's just one guy sitting there," Staś said when he returned.

"What?" Lupe said.

"There's only one musician. It's a one-man band."

Staś turned and asked everyone at the table if the locust trees were on some kind of cosmic timetable. "Do they bloom every two years, all of them? As in 1986, 1988, et cetera?"

No one seemed to know, but everyone agreed that they had never seen more locust trees in bloom, nor had the blossoms ever been as sweet-smelling as this year. Some people suggested that the trees bloomed every two years. Others thought it might be every three years.

"But it's a fact that they all bloom at once, not one of them blooms in the nonblooming years," Staś said. Several people affirmed this, and one added that the blooming of the locust trees always brings a good corn crop. Inside the house, the one-man band was playing louder now, and the music coming from the open windows took on a discordant tone. The musician was transposing upwards in half-steps, from key to key.

"But this is just like in *Pan Tadeusz* where Jankiel's music suddenly becomes discordant," Staś said. He tried to explain to his fellow guests about the progressing disharmonies that tell the story of the Massacre of Praga. The guests listened politely but didn't understand.

"Shh, Staś," Lupe said, "it's the garter." Boisterous clapping and shouting accompanied each modulation of the chord. Inside the house, the bride's dress was being raised inch by inch. Staś looked towards the house and saw the mother of the bride at the nearest window. The mother leaned out the window to talk with the guests under the tent. She was laughing. Then she drew back, and Staś saw her framed in the window, laughing, clapping, as the dress went higher and higher. Staś felt exquisite happiness. He wished the moment would last, he wanted to sit with Lupe at the wedding forever.

Soon, however, they left, after the cake. Lupe wanted to drive to a little lake not far away. They took off their clothes and swam to a raft in the middle of the lake.

"Look, Staś," Lupe said, as she clung to the raft. Between the empty oil drums that supported the raft there were twenty or thirty fish swimming in the green light.

"Beautiful," Staś said, as they both hung onto the raft, their bodies suspended, swaying in the water. They climbed onto the raft.

"Don't look at me like that," Lupe said. "You're staring at my thighs."

"I wasn't even thinking," Staś said.

On the way home, they passed the house where the guests were still dancing. The next day, Staś and Lupe found out that the guests had danced until two in the morning. As Lupe turned into their driveway, Staś said, "Lupe, let's make love now, before the bride and groom."

DUSK

"Now the love between us is so much I can almost see it," Lupe said. "It's a substance in the air."

"*Una substancia*," Staś murmured. Lupe and Staś were lying in bed in the room with the stenciled walls, which overlooked the river. At dusk, when the birds became quiet, the sound of the river entered the bedroom.

"Schooled in poetry," Staś said. "Lupe, tell me, is this love as good as when the boy came on the horse every day to see you?"

"But that was in Mexico. And Staś, you don't know how much I love you. I always tell you a love story. Tell me something from your youth."

"Water," Staś said, "I was just thinking about it. We went to Uncle Andrzej's house in the country. There was a white pump, a handpump for water. A little girl was there in white sandals. We both had on white sandals. We were four or five. We began to pump the handle together. At first no water came. Then water began to come up in snorts. Smooth silver water came rushing out in pulses, splashing all over our white sandals, splashing on the boards that covered the well."

"And did you love that little girl more than me?"

"¡Ay!, she was you, Lupe, don't you see? She'll be the flower girl at our wedding. Who are we going to invite to our wedding?"

"Well, first," Lupe said, "we must have plenty of chickens and little goats running around the yard. And the children running, trying to catch them, for the feast."

"And no conviviality of that Polish sort, where suddenly, by getting drunk, everyone becomes a good fellow and bosom buddy," Staś said emphatically. "Instead a sort of mortality and loneliness will cling to the day. Perhaps it will rain a little, or there will be a sudden wind."

· "Exactly," Lupe said. "Chickens, goats, dust, wind."

"And dogs," Staś said, "I want Potwór and Babka here. They'll sit a little distance from the wedding table, watching us eat. They're not beggars, they're distinguished sentinels. Potwór will cock his head, he'll sit with Babka and watch the whole thing, seriously."

"And Faustino will come," Lupe said, "and Gosia, Maciej, Vassily. And we'll have a few of our country neighbors. Also, my sisters, my parents."

"Yes," Staś said, "your parents. Your father will stand solemnly in his ranch hat, but he'll be the first to laugh when Vassily brings him a drink and they start to rattle away in Spanish. And Maciej will be studying the whole thing quietly, so that he will be able to tell us the story over and over again in a year's time. Dear friend. ¿Y tu madre?"

166

"And my mother," Lupe said, "will be beautiful, serene, in a flower dress. You'll bend over and kiss her, Staś. She'll embrace you, and touch your face, and say your name. You two will cry together."

THE MARRIAGE

Babka was asleep under the ash-leaf maple trees.

"And now, at last," Staś said, "we enter the river."

"And how are we going to do this?" Lupe asked. "I'm frightened."

"Look, you hold onto the beam above, on the bridge. I'll hold you up, and then you'll slide down onto my *pene*."

"*!Ay!*, Staś, I'm frightened. Are you going to stand firm under me?"

"Yes, I'm firm, my feet are on the pebbles. My feet are in the water. Here, now reach up."

Lupe reached up and grasped the steel bar beneath the bridge. Heat from the day lingered in the late afternoon. They were not cold in the river, in their nakedness. But Lupe was a little anxious.

"Suppose someone comes to visit?"

"But no one is coming to visit. Ah now, slide down."

Lupe began to slide down Staś's body. Staś held her

with the greatest of care. He put his arms lightly around her, and lowered her onto him.

"¡*Ay!*, Staś," she said. He began slowly to enter her; he wanted it to last forever: the birds, the light, the murmur of the water, the rise and fall of her breathing. He felt the reflex movement of his pelvis begin. He clasped her with his chest, his arms, his heart, his penis. He felt the water slipping by his heels.